Darby heard a splash. Her gaze followed the trail of longer, greener grass. It showed where water pooled, became a rivulet, and wandered, losing its sense of direction, then going off on a tangent before it gathered enough water to become a real stream.

Head bobbing up and down, mane flowing in waves, Hoku pulled Darby along.

At last, almost by accident, they both saw the place where the trickling water turned into a moss-silvery brook, and a creature that almost had to be a mythical beast.

Not a unicorn. There was no such thing, but Darby decided it was a creature just as rare.

Drinking with her muzzle thrust into her rosy reflection, a pink horse stood.

Check out the

Phantom Stallion

series, also by Terri Farley!

Read all the **Phantom Stallion** WILD HORSE ISLAND *adventures!*

Phantom Stallion

WILD HORSE ISLAND 3

RAIN FOREST ROSE

TERRI FARLEY

HarperTrophy®
An Imprint of HarperCollins*Publishers*

Harper Trophy® is a registered trademark
of HarperCollins Publishers.

Rain Forest Rose

Copyright © 2007 by Terri Sprenger-Farley

All rights reserved. Printed in the United States of America. No part of this book may be used or reproduced in any manner whatsoever without written permission except in the case of brief quotations embodied in critical articles and reviews. For information address HarperCollins Children's Books, a division of HarperCollins Publishers, 1350 Avenue of the Americas, New York, NY 10019.
www.harpercollinschildrens.com

Library of Congress Catalog Card Number: 2007925198
ISBN 978-0-06-088616-5

Typography by Jennifer Heuer
❖
First Harper Trophy edition, 2007

3
RAIN FOREST ROSE

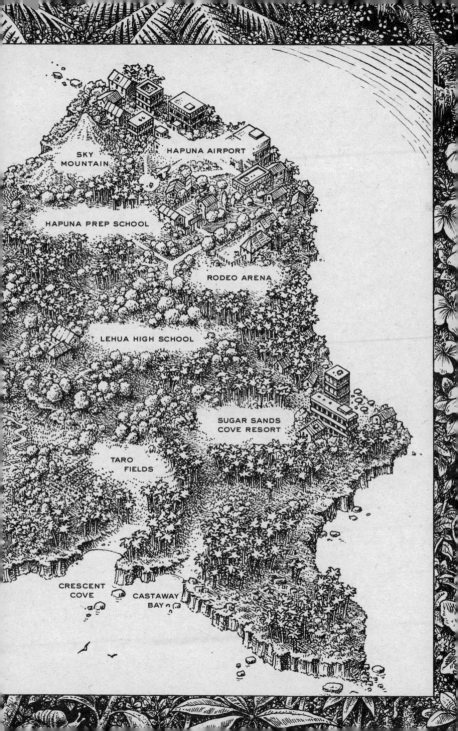

3
RAIN FOREST ROSE

Prologue

At dawn, the old woman leans on a koa wood walking stick. She looks down at the treeless circle surrounded by rain forest. In less than two years, grass, creeping plants, and saplings have reclaimed the earth that men had cleared. Vines twirl over corral bars and a wooden lean-to, the only reminders of that day.

That tragic day, she thinks, and though the ache of mourning remains, the time for blame is over.

The old woman has spent a lifetime in the rain forest and she knows the need to place blame grew out of hurt, not truth. The wild boars would have trotted through this place, on that day, even if the three riders hadn't chosen the same path.

But they did, and because they did, one life ended and two changed forever.

If a piglet hadn't stopped to stare at an insect while his littermates shuffled on and disappeared in the greenery, things might have been different. If the piglet hadn't been trapped between the cattle and the horsemen, he might not have squealed in panic, causing a boar to charge and a rose roan mare to rear from his tusked attack.

If the boar or the mare had hesitated for just three heartbeats, the paniolo would have reined the roan aside, backed her away, and laughing in relief, welcomed the lesson.

But it all happened too fast and the rearing roan crashed over backward, trapping her rider against the forest floor.

"The sun comes up, and the sun goes down," the old woman tells the owl riding her shoulder. "And what happens in between—happens."

The owl's feathered face swivels, looking back over the old woman's shoulder.

She taps her walking stick. A warm gust blows away the screams still hanging in the canopy of leaves. A second tap, and the breeze carries off the smell of hot horse flesh and the sharp rosemary scent of crushed keawe. The wind erases the pain of a dying man and the daughter at his side.

The owl lifts into the air, hangs hovering, then flaps into the wind that wraps the pink cloak around the old woman's body and her white hair around her neck.

The warm, welcome wind makes the old woman smile, because soon, this spot will not be haunted by bloody grief and grudges.

Change is on its way.

Chapter 1

"Not that it matters, but I've never camped before," Darby Carter told her grandfather, Jonah.

He balanced her backpack behind the saddle cantle, then tightened the knot holding it.

She worried a little bit about her asthma getting out of control, too, but the bulk of the inhaler in her pocket reassured her.

"You want to stay home, say so," Jonah said, but he didn't look at her.

His hands, callused from decades of work with horses, kept double-checking the job Darby had done saddling up. Now, he tested the breast collar Darby had buckled to keep Navigator's saddle from slipping on steep hills.

"No! I'm going!" Darby insisted.

Her grandfather's smile, which barely lifted the corner of his black mustache, told Darby that he knew her fretting was a habit left over from the noisy school halls, blaring freeways, and city craziness of her life before 'Iolani Ranch.

As the morning clouds parted and sunlight warmed her shoulders, Darby added to herself, *Before Hawaii.*

A low nicker made Darby watch Navigator. The Quarter Horse gelding, dark brown as coffee with rust-colored circles around his eyes, had noticed when she'd glanced down at her pocket. He flared his nostrils, sniffing to find out if she carried something for him in there.

Darby pretended to ignore Navigator, because Jonah didn't like her babying his horses. He'd told her that on her first day in Hawaii. And even though Navigator had picked her as his rider within minutes of her arrival on the ranch, the big gelding still belonged to Jonah.

"Plan on bringing your horse?" Jonah asked.

"Of course," Darby said, but she was thinking, *My horse.*

No other words could kindle a glow inside her like those two.

Well, maybe one: *Hoku.*

Even though she was a mustang from the Nevada rangelands, Darby had named her sorrel filly Hoku, the Hawaiian word for "star." She was named for the white marking on her chest but, Darby thought proudly, her horse was a star in other ways. Since coming to Hawaii, the filly had not only braved a long swim in the sea and survived; she'd also chased off a wild stallion set on kidnapping her for his herd.

That first day, Jonah had also told her that the best way to bond with her mustang filly was to set out into the rain forest—alone.

The thought still gave her chills, but so far, everything Jonah had told her about horses had turned out to be true. This morning she would prove she trusted her grandfather as much as he trusted her.

Jonah had given her a map. He'd ride partway out with her to the forest, and then leave her to go on alone. Astride Navigator and leading Hoku, she'd find the camp marked on the map. It would have a corral for Hoku, a lean-to for Darby to sleep in, and a nearby stream of fresh water. Once she found it, she'd send Navigator home. Then she and Hoku would stay for a week.

We can do it, Darby thought.

"That's good." Jonah faced his own horse now, testing the latigo and buckles on the tack of his gray, Kona.

What's good? Darby wondered. The way her mind had darted around, she'd totally lost track of their conversation.

Jonah looked over Kona's back. Brown skin

crinkled at the corners of Jonah's eyes and he tilted his head so that she saw the gray hair at his temples.

At least he didn't look impatient with her, Darby thought, but then she realized her grandfather was gazing past her.

"Here comes the roughrider. Already dropped food out there for you." Jonah gave a wry smile as Cade rode up.

Wearing short leather chaps streaked with green stains, Cade swung in the saddle in time with his horse's high spirits. With his tugged-low hat, rawhide rope, and dark green poncho, Cade looked all business. But not Joker. The black-spattered Appaloosa danced as if he were setting out on an adventure, instead of coming back from one.

"I left your sleeping bag and your food up there," Cade said.

"Good thing he can see in the dark," Jonah told Darby. "Before dawn, that forest is black as the inside of a cow."

"Thanks, Cade," Darby said.

Still in the saddle, Cade shrugged off Jonah's compliment and her thanks.

At fifteen, Cade was only two years older than Darby, but her grandfather's unofficially adopted son was a world of experience ahead of her.

Still, the one thing Darby did best in all the world was learn.

Jonah's eyes flicked toward Hoku's corral. Before

he could rush her, Darby sprinted away.

"I'm getting Hoku. Be right back," she shouted over her shoulder.

As she jogged, Darby took deep, testing breaths. Her asthma had improved since she'd come to Hawaii. Oxygen didn't grate through her lungs and she felt no catch in her chest. The remote island of Moku Lio Hihiu had zero air pollution compared to Southern California.

At the sound of Darby's boots, Hoku bolted away from the fence, then stretched her neck high and higher still to see over the top rail.

"Good morning, beauty," Darby called.

The filly stared through the creamy ripples of her forelock. Sunlight turned her brown eyes amber. She looked as wild as the first day Darby had seen her galloping across a snowy plain, drawing away from the helicopter chasing her.

"Hoku," Darby said, smooching, and the filly's wild expression was replaced by impatience.

Hoku arched her golden neck and pawed three rapid strokes.

"Were you afraid I was going to leave you behind when I rode out on Navigator?"

Carefully sliding open the new bolt on Hoku's corral, Darby slipped inside carrying a tangerine-and-white-striped lead rope.

In mock fear, the filly shied away.

Hoku's coat shone with good health. Even though

Jonah said it would take a few more months for the filly to recover from her journey from Nevada to Hawaii, Darby couldn't imagine any horse could be more beautiful.

On her shipping papers, Hoku had been described as a sorrel in one place and a chestnut in another.

To Darby, Hoku looked like living fire. Flashes of flame red outlined the muscles surging beneath the filly's golden skin. Copper glints shone on her legs. Sparks crackled in her flaxen mane.

Hoku stopped, shook her head, and snorted, promising Darby that today she wouldn't be hard to catch.

But Darby had been fooled before, and she didn't have time to calm Hoku if the filly changed her mind.

Darby came to Hoku slowly, with one hand held out to pet the filly if she stepped forward.

She didn't. So, instead of approaching from the front, Darby slid along her horse's side. The filly's body was warm and vibrating with energy.

"Pretty girl," Darby praised, then snapped the lead on Hoku's halter.

Hoku trusted Darby more than she did any other human, but the filly's wild heritage could be traced to horses called "throwbacks" and "renegades." She'd already hurt Cade—out of fear, not malice—and Darby wasn't taking the chance of spooking her horse.

Hoku lifted each hoof in prancing perfection as they moved out of the corral and back toward Jonah.

Her ears tilted forward, curious about the group of people ahead. Even from this distance, Darby recognized her friend Megan by her athletic build and cherry Coke–colored hair, and Auntie Cathy.

Darby had described Auntie Cathy to her own mother as Megan's mom, the resident cook, and general ranch manager. But the woman with the messy brown-blond bob was also the widow of a paniolo who'd been Jonah's right-hand man. Auntie Cathy mothered everyone on the ranch, and she knew more about 'Iolani Ranch than anyone except Jonah.

But Hoku wasn't snorting at Megan or Auntie Cathy.

The filly's flattened ears signaled the nearness of a male. She had good reasons to dislike men, and she was warning Cade not to ride any closer.

Cade stopped Joker out of the reach of Hoku's hooves and teeth, but the filly protested with a squeal when Cade leaned down from his saddle to say, "Hope you're not afraid of spiders."

Darby missed a step and tripped into Megan. The other girl steadied her and reached a comforting hand toward Hoku.

"Oh, stop it, Cade," Megan snapped.

"Most of the ones out there are just happy-face spiders." Auntie Cathy dismissed Cade's warning with an indulgent smile.

"Happy-face spiders?" Darby echoed, then looked at Jonah with raised eyebrows.

"No bigger than your little fingernail," Jonah confirmed. When Darby glanced down at her hands, he gave a short bark of laughter.

"They have markings that look like smiles, but they're all a little bit different," Megan explained. Then, hands on hips, she added, "And I think they're cute."

"Not like cane spiders," Cade said in an offhanded manner that contradicted his satisfied expression.

Darby's first thought was of candy canes, and she said, "They don't sound so bad."

"They're gross. They hide in groves of sugar cane," Megan said, "so you probably won't see them by the corral, but sometimes they migrate. When we were in town once, we saw them march across the street in waves." Megan rubbed her arms with a shudder.

Darby's imagination displayed an undulating carpet of tarantulas, before she could remind herself that she was not afraid of spiders. All creatures were fascinating. She was proud she'd never reacted to snakes and spiders with stereotyped girliness, and she wasn't about to give Cade the satisfaction of seeing her cringe.

"Thanks for the heads-up," Darby told Cade, then tightened her long black ponytail.

At the same time, Hoku stepped closer to her, and Jonah reprimanded, "Keep both hands on that lead rope."

Darby did, and then, before Jonah could tell her to make Hoku back up, she did that, too.

Rules for horses were straightforward and simple with Jonah. If a horse came at you or walked away without permission, you ordered him or her to back up a few steps.

"Back," Darby said, but Hoku just switched her glare from Cade to Jonah, until Darby flicked the end of the lead rope toward the filly's white-starred chest.

Lifting her chin in understanding, Hoku took a step back.

"One more," Darby said and lifted her own chin to acknowledge the filly's response.

"Good," Jonah said. "Now she remembers who's in charge."

"No fair having Hoku stomp them," Cade muttered. "Killing spiders is bad luck."

"So is sleeping with spiders," Megan pointed out, "so shake out your sleeping bag before you bed down every night."

"Enough," Auntie Cathy said, then gave Darby a one-armed hug. "Darby will do just fine."

"Time to go," Jonah said, reining Kona away from them all.

Darby put her boot toe in Navigator's stirrup, but

hesitated before bouncing up into the saddle.

Megan was beside her, whispering, "Let me slip this in here."

"What is it?" Darby asked as Megan unzipped an outside pocket on Darby's backpack.

Megan pushed a small brown sack inside, then zipped it closed again. "Something you can use when you're working with Hoku. It'll get her used to weird things. My dad"—Megan's voice wavered, reminding Darby her friend's father had only been dead for a year—"had me do this with my horse. It worked really well." Megan cleared her throat. "Anyhow, it's fun."

"Thanks," Darby said, then asked, "which horse?"

For a second, she thought Megan hadn't heard her, but when she started to ask again, Megan said, "Later."

"Promise?" Darby asked, and she wouldn't have noticed Auntie Cathy was following their quiet exchange, except that the woman looked away when Megan rolled her eyes in pretend exasperation, then nodded.

"Watch out for wild pigs," Auntie Cathy put in, as Darby gave Hoku's lead rope one wrap around her hand. "Darby?"

Auntie Cathy's voice was insistent and sharper than usual.

"I'll watch for them," Darby promised. "Even

though I didn't get the pig-tracking class you gave Kit."

"You'll know them when you see them," Auntie Cathy said.

Darby didn't try to analyze the woman's forced lightness.

Jonah was getting ahead of her, so Darby swung into the saddle and nudged Navigator with her heels.

"Bye," Megan called, and Darby looked back over her shoulder to see Cade and Megan wave at exactly the same time.

Darby lifted her reins, telling Navigator to catch up with Jonah as he passed Sun House. The gelding lengthened his stride and Hoku picked her feet up cautiously, following a path of her own, at the end of the tangerine-and-white rope.

As they descended the bluff and crossed the broodmare pasture, Jonah sounded like a coach before a big game, jamming last-minute advice into her brain.

"Work on her head-shyness however you want. You'll build a relationship as you cure the problem," he said. "You've made a start, but halfway won't cut it. It's a dangerous vice. You're goin' nowhere, if you don't fix that."

Hoku didn't have vices, Darby thought. Her head-shyness was a logical reaction to being beaten.

"Down deep, this filly hasn't forgiven you for stealing her freedom."

Darby couldn't contradict him, because sometimes she thought the same thing. She was working at giving Hoku the best life a captive mustang could have. But sometimes Hoku stared west for motionless minutes, only to turn back to Darby with unforgiving eyes.

The filly was learning to trust, but she still yearned for the boundless range of home.

Darby looked back over her shoulder. Hoku raised her head to return the girl's gaze.

Maybe someday, Darby told Hoku silently, *you'll run as far and fast as you want, and still come back to me.*

But they had a long way to go before that happened. As Darby thought of schooling Hoku, she remembered the bag Megan had slipped into her backpack. Then she recalled what Megan had said about her own horse.

"Which horse is Megan's?" Darby asked.

"What do you mean?" Jonah replied, without looking at her.

"She told me she was training a horse with her dad. Was it Biscuit?" Darby knew Megan's dad, Ben, had ridden the buckskin named Biscuit.

"No, Megan had a wild horse. A pink one."

"Pink?" Darby was surprised such a thing existed.

"A rose roan, they call 'em, but yeah, Tango pretty much looked pink."

Tango. Darby pictured Megan on a high-stepping

mare with hooves clattering like castanets.

"Was she sold?" Darby asked, but Jonah was shaking his head before she finished.

"Megan's horse was in a bad accident."

"What happened?" Darby pressed him.

"You know on the map, it shows the *kipuka*? It's sort of an island within an island, yeah? Lava flows around a piece of earth and a rain forest grows up on that earth in the middle. This *kipuka* you're going to," Jonah explained, "you've got to cross some *'a'a*—the rough kind of lava. After the accident, she took off that way. We found blood," he said grimly.

"Why didn't someone go after her?" Darby gasped.

"It was the same day Ben died. We kinda had our hands full," Jonah said.

Darby sucked in a breath, glad that Jonah hadn't let her rattle on thoughtlessly.

"After things settled down, Mekana said to let the mare go back to the wild. She didn't want to ride ever again, she told everyone."

Jonah gave her a grateful smile after he said that, crediting Darby with Megan's return to riding, so Darby didn't say what she was thinking.

You let her have her way? Jonah must be leaving something out.

If Megan didn't want to ride, if she'd lost her nerve after her father died in a horseback accident, okay. But finding the horse—especially if it was injured—was the humane thing to do. Besides, every animal on the ranch was valued in dollars. There must be more to Tango's escape and Ben's death than Jonah was telling her.

They rode in silence until Jonah muttered, "Look at that." He pointed out a haphazard gouge through the grass, cut through to the damp earth. "Pigs. Like Cathy told you, be careful."

"I will."

"And if you think you hear them, you probably do."

"Okay," she said. "But I'm not such a city girl that I wouldn't recognize a pig."

"These are different from pigs in kids' books," Jonah said. "They're not cute. They gobble up birds. They're bristly and black. They go rooting day or night."

The gash through the grass had looked like a furrow dug by a drunken plowman. Swiveling in her saddle, Darby looked back and asked, "Why do they do that?"

"Looking for food, like the rest of us," Jonah said, "but they're a menace. How'd you like to be on a running horse when he stepped in a rip like that?"

Darby didn't want to think about it. She was still awkward riding a horse at any gait. It would be bad news if Navigator stepped into a hole that deep.

"I'll watch the ground," Darby promised.

"You watch the space between your horses' ears,"

Jonah corrected. "He'll keep watch of the ground."
Jonah looked over his shoulder as Hoku shied at a
swooping yellow bird.

When Hoku felt his eyes on her, she flattened her
ears.

She pays such close attention, Darby thought. *Even a
beginner like me should be able to teach her.*

Jonah squinted toward the rain forest ahead. "I
wouldn't let you go out here if I thought there was
any danger. Much safer than crossing a street in
Pacific Pinnacles." He pronounced the name of
Darby's hometown in California in a pointed way.
"You won't get run down by some movie star's limou-
sine."

"It's not that kind of a neighborhood—" Darby
began, but Jonah cut her off.

"Just stay back, out of their way, and they'll leave
you be. Don't let that filly go after one, either."

"Would a horse chase a pig?" she asked incredu-
lously.

"It's in her nature to protect you."

"I thought you said she hadn't forgiven me for
trying to tame her," Darby said.

"All animals are walking contradictions. Horses
and humans are born that way. Fierce and gentle.
Wild and protective. Not many have the brains to
back up their actions." Jonah studied Hoku. When
the filly snorted, one side of Jonah's black mustache
lifted with his smile. "That's why they need us."

"I think she knows more about the wild than—"

"No." Jonah halted Kona across the path and pointed his index finger at Darby as she stopped Navigator. "You know more, and this is why you're going out here." He shook the finger three or four times, then drew a deep breath, and when he talked again, the irritation in his voice had faded.

"Remember I told you about *mana*?" Jonah asked.

Darby remembered when Jonah had made the strong stallion Luna behave for the farrier, just by sheer force of will. Jonah had said that was mana versus mana, but it hadn't meant much more to her than any of his other Hawaiian teachings. She was interested, of course, but he expected her to keep track of so much.

Still, Darby nodded.

"Well, there are two kinds of mana. One's your own power, a strength of spirit you're born with. The other mana is what you've learned from the mouths of others."

Jonah let her mull that over for a few seconds before he asked, "Which mana is stronger in you?"

Self-conscious and not really sure what he wanted from her, Darby shrugged her shoulders up until they almost touched her earlobes. Her mother had once told her she looked like a turtle withdrawing into its shell when she did that. Now, that's how she felt.

"I don't know."

"The learning from others—you're good at that, and you know it," he said.

"Yeah."

"And you're particular about who you believe. That's good," Jonah said, and then he glanced down at her wrist. "But that ancient necklace you found. No one told you it had power, and yet you sensed it."

"I only wore it as a good-luck charm," Darby protested.

"And once you learned it belonged in the *ali'i*'s cave, how did you feel?"

"I wanted to put it back—"

"Because you felt superstitious? Or you were afraid you'd get in trouble?" Jonah asked her.

"No! Because it was the right thing to do."

"That's your own mana," Jonah said, as if it was obvious. "Like the way you bonded with the filly."

Darby opened her mouth to remind him, again, that he thought the filly still held a grudge.

"Who does that, Darby? Lies down in the snow with a wild horse, and stands up its best friend. You have a lot of pals, yeah, in California, who do that all the time?"

"No, but it's not like magic—"

"Mana's not magic. It's an instinct, a silent power, an understanding. You have it for horses, and so do I. But you don't trust your mana. I do."

Once more, Darby remembered the stallion Luna

facing Jonah. Like silent thunder, the man's will had rolled over the horse. And Luna had obeyed without hesitation.

"So, when I come back from the rain forest," Darby spoke slowly, thinking before each word, "how are you going to tell if I figured out my two manas?"

"This isn't school. There's no test." Jonah smiled. "Or if there is, you'll be the one to recognize it. Not me."

My "instinctive" mana and my "what I've learned from others" mana, Darby thought as they rode on. *Okay, that shouldn't be too hard.*

"When you get where you're going," Jonah said over his shoulder, "put Navigator's reins up and turn him loose with a slap on the rump. He'll head for home. And Cade will be bringing you more food and checking on you."

"Okay," Darby said. But as the vegetation narrowed the path, she realized Jonah's instructions probably meant they'd reached the spot where he'd turn around and go back to the ranch.

They hadn't ridden that far. Surely, she thought, as her mind darted back to Megan's lost horse, someone should have seen Tango in almost two years. And even in wild Hawaii, shouldn't the police have looked over the scene of a sudden death? Maybe they had. Maybe Jonah didn't want her to hear the grisly details of a paniolo's death, when she was still just learning to ride.

"This is where I leave you," Jonah said, halting Kona at the gate out of the broodmare pasture.

"Okay." Darby heard the faintness of her own voice as she pictured herself riding on with the two horses. Then walking on, with one.

"Thanks, Grandpa." Darby surprised even herself by saying it, and she would have hugged him if she could have done so without falling off her horse. "I'll do my best."

Jonah made a *hmph*ing noise, before he said, "There's mostly geldings in Pearl Pasture."

A twitch of reins made Kona sidestep until Jonah could open the gate for Darby to ride through. "Being the tomboy she is, Hoku won't likely flirt with 'em, but she might want to join in a run. Don't let her. Stop her before she jerks you off Navigator's back, yeah?"

"I will," Darby said. She gave a quiet cluck to encourage Hoku to follow Navigator through the gate. Hoku came along, but her narrowed eyes said she did it because Darby asked her to, not because she trusted Jonah enough to turn her tail on him.

"Gonna be one strong mare," Jonah said approvingly, and then he made the one-handed gesture with three fingers folded inside and waggled it from side to side. Megan had told her it was called *shaka* and it meant "hi" or "good-bye" or any kind of greeting in between.

Holding Hoku's rope tight in her right hand, Darby returned the gesture with her left and made Jonah chuckle.

Jonah's laughter still echoed in Darby's ears long after the gate to Pearl Pasture was locked behind her.

Chapter 2

When Darby first noticed she was wheezing, she was glad there was no way for her mom to give her one of the stinging injections she'd learned to administer. There'd be no late-night trip to the urgent-care clinic, either, and though she probably shouldn't have felt relieved by that, Darby did.

Besides, she had the medihaler in her pocket, just in case. The tight feeling in Darby's chest vanished as a beautiful troop of horses, led by a palomino, suddenly appeared.

Hoku gave a neigh. Her head bobbed and she pulled at the rope as snorts answered her.

"Oh my gosh," Darby whispered to Navigator, though the gelding didn't act as awed as she was or as curious as Hoku. "Who are you guys?" she whispered to the new herd.

Darby knew the answer. They were in Pearl Pasture, so these were two- and three-year-olds in training, but she kept talking to keep the horses' attention.

"They're just about your age," Darby told Hoku.

With her brown eyes fixed on the other horses, Hoku weaved from one side of the path to the other at a shifting gait.

The horses of Pearl Pasture pranced with exuberance. Delighted to have visitors, they pressed close to Navigator and Hoku.

Careful, Darby reminded herself. Jonah had warned her not to let Hoku jerk her out of the saddle.

Steadiness on horseback wasn't something she could always count on, and she had the bruises to prove it.

Darby watched Hoku for signs that she might lunge. At the same time, she imitated Jonah's matter-of-fact way of talking to horses.

"Get back, guys," Darby told the young geldings. "We're following this path to a clearing. Then we're turning right and going to the *kipuka.* Just passing through."

The horses took no notice of the directions she'd memorized from Jonah's map, but they didn't correct her pronunciation, either.

She admired their wet, healthy coats. Bays, a

black, and a blue roan she recognized as Buckin'
Baxter surrounded them, but the palomino kept forg-
ing to the front.

All at once, Darby's back twisted, then snapped
up straight, and her teeth clacked together. As the
faint, red trail widened, Navigator burst from a walk
into a full lope.

"How'd you skip over a trot?" Darby yelped, and
then she gasped.

For a few strides, Hoku had kept up with
Navigator, but now the filly had noticed the young
geldings falling in behind. She wanted the comfort of
the herd.

Hoku balked.

Navigator kept moving.

Between them, the horses stretched Darby's arm.
She pictured a cartoon character's arm lengthening
like rubber.

"Whoa!" she shouted, and then, tightening her
reins with her other hand, she yelled, "Hoku!"

Darby figured it was her commanding voice, or
the suddenly narrowing trail—not any kind of
mana—that made the horses obey. Whatever caused
it, Darby was relieved that Navigator didn't bolt into
a gallop, but slowed to a hammering trot, and Hoku
mirrored his gait.

"Good boy," she congratulated the coffee-colored
gelding. As the young horses caught up, he stayed in
the lead, changing his trot into a floating gait she

didn't recognize. "Really good boy."

Navigator's hooves sounded like faint applause on the forest floor. And Hoku's hooves were their echo. Darby sighed and forgot about her arm as she drifted along.

She might have been riding in a dream, until Hoku gave a pleased buck and Darby lost her left stirrup.

"No," Darby snapped. Scuffing her boot back into place broke the spell, and Navigator returned to his uneasy jog.

The other horses' glossy shoulders jostled them, but Darby heard something beyond the hoofbeats and rushing leaves.

What was that sound? Darby wished she could prick her ears up like the horses. Was someone talking?

Voices on the wind spoke to Darby.

I've been here before, she thought.

The jungle left just a single-file passageway for the horses. The geldings took their cues from Navigator, but even as they settled into a flat-footed walk, their tails twitched and their forelocks flew. They snuffled, testing the air currents.

The horses' multicolored backs moved so slowly, Darby counted them.

"One, two, three—" Darby broke off when Navigator crowded past the black horse and pinned Darby's left leg between the two warm bodies.

Alarm made her pulse speed up and the tightness in her chest grew worse, but only for a second. Hoku mirrored Navigator's free-striding walk and Darby felt like one of the herd. She lowered her head from drooping branches as Navigator shoved ahead of the black, a bay, then forced the blue roan to give way.

Scarlet blooms like those she'd seen in the waterfall valley whipped Darby's hair. She ducked as they rushed past.

Wind kept the tunnel of trees in motion. Maybe a storm was brewing, she thought, watching green stems bend under leaves that looked like inside-out umbrellas.

Hoku and I came this way, finding our way home from Crescent Beach, Darby realized.

Ahead, leaves streaked with salmon-orange stroked the palomino's flanks.

He kicked, then nipped at the spot the leaf had tickled, and Darby, Navigator, and Hoku went ahead.

All at once, the wind stopped. The forest seemed to hold its breath.

Darby tightened her reins. Navigator halted. He arched his neck, stamped, and blew, but Hoku didn't make a sound.

Darby glanced over her shoulder. The filly looked hypnotized.

By what? Darby wondered, until she followed the mustang's gaze.

A dazzling sunbeam stabbed through the trees. It shone on a cottage.

Navigator bowed his head three times, asking her to loosen the reins.

"Sorry, boy." Darby's voice might have boomed from a loudspeaker.

It had rained more here than at the ranch, she noticed. A falling leaf plopped onto a deep puddle.

A metallic ping made Darby look back to the clearing.

How many times had she had dreamed of rain dropping from that rust-red roof? As many times as she'd seen that white curtain billowing out that window. But she'd only *dreamed* of the cottage in the clearing, and now she was wide awake.

Darby tapped Navigator's sides with her heels. She had to know what waited behind that door!

When it opened, not creaking, but swinging wide on well-oiled hinges, Darby had already slid down from Navigator, still clinging to Hoku's lead rope.

Silhouetted in the doorway, the woman in the long dress could have been any age, but when she stepped into the sunlight, Darby felt like she'd ridden into the future.

The oval face, heavy brows, scarf-bound hair, and startling smile could have belonged to her mother, grown old.

Or me! Darby jerked back in recognition. Though the eyes watching her were brown, not blue, the face before Darby looked an awful lot like the one she saw in the mirror.

"Aloha, Darby."

The melodious voice should have come from someone big and jolly, but the arms that swooped around Darby were thin inside the floating pink dress.

"Aloha," the woman repeated as she kissed Darby's cheeks. "I'm your *tutu*."

As she held Darby out at arm's length to look at her, Darby felt at home, as if she'd always known this woman everyone called Tutu, as if she were their great-grandmother as well. People on 'Iolani Ranch spoke of Tutu with reverence, mentioning her healing skills and insight, acting as if living in the jungle, alone, was the way of such wise women.

And I know why, Darby thought with a dizzy smile. The loneliness she'd felt since leaving home faded under this outpouring of love from a total stranger who reminded her so strongly of her mother.

Hoku hadn't moved or made a sound. Anxiously, Darby glanced back. The filly had every sense focused on the human before her, but she wasn't braced to bolt. She looked—Darby searched her vocabulary—peaceful.

"I dreamed of being here," Darby admitted.

She couldn't help it. Instinct told her that her great-grandmother wouldn't label her a nutcase, but she hadn't meant to let the words just tumble out.

"And I dreamed of having you here," her great-grandmother said. "You and your horse with the golden tail."

Darby broke out in goose bumps.

"You really dreamed of Hoku?"

"Dreams, visions . . ." Tutu wafted her hand through the air. "They're very much alike."

"They are?" Darby asked. "I have dreams every night, but I've never had a vision."

"They're not so mysterious," Tutu said with a mild smile. "But if no one around you feels anything when you do, or if they're destructive, you're not having a vision. You're just—" She broke off to tap her temple. *"Hewa-hewa."*

Darby grinned. She didn't need a Hawaiian translator for that. It had to mean *crazy.*

What she did need was a puff of her asthma inhaler. It was a terrible time to be wheezing. She felt like she could really talk with Tutu and ask her things—about her mother and Jonah, about Ben Kato's death and Megan's lost horse—but Darby could barely catch her breath. Having a long chat was out of the question.

"Yam root tea will help your breathing," Tutu told her. "I'll make you some."

"I have medicine," Darby gasped, but when she patted her pocket, it was empty.

No! She stuck her hand all the way to the bottom of her pocket. She checked the other one. There was nothing there, either. The inhaler was gone, and she really didn't want to backtrack along the trail looking for it.

"Yam root tea?" Darby asked. She was willing to try anything to keep from going back.

"I'm an expert after making it all those years for Jonah."

"That's right." Darby forced out the words, remembering asthma was something she shared with her grandfather.

"I plant yams every other year," Tutu said, then recited, "root toward the mountain, root toward the sea, root to the windward, root to the lee."

Darby thought the rhyme was another link to her family. She often used rhymes to help her remember things she was studying. Like *i* before *e*, except after *c*, she thought.

How cool was it that her great-grandmother was using such memory tricks in Hawaii?

"Just let your horses go. He'll stay, won't you, boy?" Tutu cupped her empty hands and Navigator nuzzled them in greeting. "It's not the first time Navigator's brought me company."

"But Hoku . . . ?" Darby couldn't think what to do with her filly, but she didn't have the breath to explain how much she didn't want to stay outside and hold the filly's lead rope.

Still, she hadn't yet trained Hoku to stand while tied. A nightmarish image of Hoku flinging her neck back, trying to break loose, invaded Darby's mind.

"She leads well," Tutu said, and her tone sounded like a hint.

Darby nodded, then wondered what would happen if she tied Hoku's rope to Navigator's saddle horn. Darby made a loop in the end of the rope, stood on tiptoe to reach the horn, and flipped it over.

"Is that safe?" Darby gasped the three words.

"Here, it is," Tutu said.

Darby rubbed her breastbone as if that would loosen her tight chest, but of course it didn't. It wasn't terrible pain, but each breath felt like the creak of an unoiled door hinge in a horror movie.

Darby watched Hoku. The sorrel didn't seem to notice she was restrained. She fell to grazing beside Navigator.

A cacophony of brass, glass, and bamboo wind chimes drew Darby's eyes back to the front porch of the cottage. Her great-grandmother wasn't there. She must have gone inside to make tea, Darby thought, so Darby followed her.

Darby remembered to take off her shoes before going inside. She'd been so embarrassed when she hadn't noticed the custom the first night she'd entered Sun House.

One step inside this house made her glad she was barefoot.

Tutu's cottage was carpeted with a woven rug that felt nubby and smooth, like intertwined sea grasses.

The room smelled of herbs and honey, which made her certain that she'd be breathing more freely soon.

A copper teakettle sat on an old-fashioned stove in the corner. A plume of steam already rose from its spout.

Darby didn't have much faith in home remedies, but Tutu moved with the competence of a pharmacist. She reached up to one of the shelves lining the cottage walls, took down a glass jar, and held it at eye level before measuring dried leaves into a green teapot.

Vapor clouded the corner as Tutu poured boiling water into the pot.

"Now that will steep," Tutu said, then gestured widely. "Please, have a look around."

Darby laced her fingers together behind her back, feeling awkward. A glance showed her no television, telephone, or computer, but she noticed a lei-draped, black-and-white photograph of a man. He looked a lot like Jonah.

"Your great-grandfather," Tutu said, as if she was introducing them. "A scallywag and a smuggler with a million schemes, but I've always had a soft spot in my heart for pirates."

Darby didn't know what to say to that. It was a strangely, well, romantic thing to hear from an old lady.

"I love my little house," Tutu said, looking around.

"Me too," Darby managed.

"It was a sugar plantation house at one time. Housing for the workers, not the bosses," Tutu said as Darby looked around. "It had neighbors, but after the tsunami, only this one was left."

"Tsunami?" Darby said. They had earthquakes in Southern California, but Darby thought tsunamis were worse, kind of like an earthquake and flood combined.

And then her gaze settled on Tutu. Was it safe for a woman of her years to live all alone in a tsunami zone?

"It happened nearly a hundred years ago," Tutu reassured Darby, as if she'd spoken her concern. "But these are young islands—formed by fire, shaped by earthquakes, floods, and yes, tsunamis, and I'd live here even if such events happened every week."

"Why?" Darby asked.

"Civilization has nothing to offer me. What do I need with video games when I'm entertained by the weather, plants, and animals? Why should I carry a cell phone when visitors stop in with the news? I don't even need a doorbell. The birds told me you were walking the path to my door."

As Tutu moved to pour their tea into mugs, she waved Darby toward a wooden table and chairs.

"Sit down. After you've had some tea, if you have the breath for it, I'd love for you to tell me how your sweet mother is doing. I miss her."

Darby settled into a chair, feeling strangely at

home. White curtains framed her view of Navigator and Hoku, still side by side, and she heard their teeth grinding grass.

As she tried to come up with things Tutu would want to hear about Mom, Darby's eyes took in the bolts of colorful cloth on one shelf and the books on another. Small trees grew in pottery bowls. A blue glass jar held water and stones. A green one was half full of shells. Growing plants sent roots among the stones and shells, and vines cascaded to the floor.

"You know, she used to ride out and visit me like this," Tutu said as she set a saucer of lemon slices and a honeypot on the table. "But it's been, oh, fifteen years or more."

Darby took a sip from the pottery cup as soon as her great-grandmother handed it to her. She tried to picture her mother riding out here as she'd just done. The image was hazy, but the idea made her happy.

As Tutu sat down to drink her own tea, Darby said, "She looks like you."

Tutu didn't sound surprised. "Kealoha women keep their family resemblance, no matter the men we marry."

Transfixed by the tendrils of steam swirling up from the tea, Darby described her mother's roller-coaster acting career, her divorce, and her longing to live at the beach, even though it meant home was on a seedy side street that smelled not of salt air, but of Dumpsters and fish bones.

Tutu soaked up the information, then said, "And the best thing is that Ellen sent you home."

"I don't know how she ever left," Darby confessed.

"She'd say she was driven away. Jonah would say she ran." Tutu shrugged, but she put everything so simply and clearly, Darby wished she'd had Tutu to come home to every day after school.

"Why haven't I ever met you?" Darby asked.

"I knew you'd come out in your own good time," Tutu said.

"I mean, ever," Darby insisted. "Kids with great-grandmothers usually know about them."

"What did your mother say about that?"

Darby didn't feel mad about her mother's secrecy anymore. In fact, she gave a breathy laugh as she explained, "Mom said she knew if she told me that the rest of my family lived on a horse ranch in Hawaii, I'd never shut up about it until I got to go there."

Tutu chuckled. "And was she right? Do you like 'Iolani Ranch?"

"I love it!" Darby couldn't keep her arms from opening wide as if she'd embrace everything around her. Finally she put her hands back on the table and folded them.

"I love it, too." Tutu patted Darby's hand. "But tell me about yourself, Darby. What else do you love?"

Darby drew a deep breath. The tea had beaten

her asthma, but her list was still short. "Books, horses, and my family."

It had been easier to talk about her flamboyant mother.

"Friends?" Tutu urged her to go on.

"Sure," Darby said. "My best friend at home is Heather. We're both nerds."

Tutu smiled in a way that made it clear she understood, then asked, "And here?"

"I like Megan and Cade."

"Wonderful children, both of them," Tutu said.

"Yes, but—" Darby stopped, shaking her head.

Tutu waited. Darby could see this warm conversation would stall out if she didn't say what she'd been about to.

"Well, it's none of my business, and no one seems worried about it except for me, but why does Megan hate Cade?"

"Hate?"

"Well, she told me I wouldn't like him—not *like*, like, but you know, as a friend—if I knew what he was capable of." Darby saw Tutu's eyebrows lift, but she said nothing. "And then there's something going on with the death of Megan's father. I don't want to be nosy, but why would she just let her horse go?

"It doesn't make sense," Darby went on, "but it's not a good way to start a friendship, to go prying into someone's private life. . . ." Darby's voice trailed off.

She stared at the greenish tea leaves in the bottom of her cup.

"Every family has its secrets," Tutu said. "And even if the Katos aren't of the same blood as us, they are family. Ben would have taken over the ranch from Jonah —"

"That's another thing — I mean, excuse me," Darby said, covering her mouth.

"Please, go ahead."

"Why is Jonah so worried about someone taking over the ranch from him? He's not that old, but I've heard about" — Darby looked up at the cottage rafters and counted off Kimo, Pani, Ben, and Cade on her fingers — "*four* men who were supposed to take over the ranch from him."

Tutu made a dismissing gesture, then asked, "Has no one told you about Ben's death?"

"Not really," Darby said.

"On the day Ben died, he and Cade were moving cattle from the forest to the ranch, and Megan had tagged along," Tutu began.

Darby felt as if she'd been socked in the stomach. "She was there when her father died?"

"Oh, yes," Tutu said.

"And what happened?"

"Wild pigs somehow got underfoot. The horses spooked, and Ben fell."

Darby was frustrated by the way Tutu shared

only the bare facts. She didn't explain how an experienced paniolo fell off his horse, or say why Cade and Ben had herded the cattle into the midst of wild pigs.

It didn't make sense, Darby thought. She'd been warned repeatedly about wild pigs, so they must be common. Hawaiian horsemen would know what to watch for, wouldn't they?

"And Megan—"

"Was with her father when he died," Tutu said.

Darby held her hands over her eyes for a few seconds. She wasn't mourning Ben Kato, a man she'd never met. She was putting herself in Megan's place and thinking of her own father, back on the mainland.

Darby gave her head a quick shake. She pictured Megan slipping down from the saddle, running to her father's side, not caring what became of her green-broke filly.

"And that's when she lost her horse?" Darby guessed.

"Yes."

It sounded as if Ben's death was just a terrible accident. So, what grudge was Megan holding against Cade?

"But Megan . . ." Darby tried to put her thoughts in order before going on. "Does she think Cade could have saved Ben? Or is it just easier to be mad instead of heartsick over her dad?"

"I wasn't there," Tutu said, "but I helped later. No

one could have saved Ben after the horse fell on top of him."

Darby tried to accept that and start a new conversation, but as long as Tutu was putting up with her curiosity, she had to ask one more thing.

Tutu hadn't been there.

Jonah hadn't been there.

But Megan had been, and her words about Cade pounded back at Darby: *You don't know what he's capable of.*

"Tutu, could Cade have—totally without meaning to—caused the accident?"

"That," Tutu said, "I do not know."

Chapter 3

Tutu left Darby brooding at the table.

Returning to her kitchen corner, Tutu said, "It's lunchtime. Late for it, really. Before time gets away from us and you have to make camp in the dark, you'll need some food in your stomach."

"Thank you," Darby said. She noticed again how much Tutu resembled her mother. Except, Darby thought, smiling, Ellen Kealoha Carter joked that she aspired to be "high maintenance."

"Did my mom like the ranch?" Darby asked.

"She loved it," Tutu insisted. "And now that you're here, I think she'll return."

"I don't know," Darby said. Her mother was pretty stubborn, and she had kept her promise not to return to Hawaii for well over a decade.

"Wait and see," Tutu said, arranging something that looked like a vegetable steamer on the stove. "Everyone who's lived on that ranch knows it's a treasure, and we've been very fortunate to keep it."

Tutu left cooking and returned to the table. Darby looked up and met her great-grandmother's brown eyes. They looked misty for a few seconds, then cleared as she tapped her index finger on the table.

"This land is part of us, no matter what. When one of my children went with the old ways and one with the new, I split the land between them."

"You split the ranch?" Darby repeated.

"Yes, I simply drew a line" — Tutu slid her fingertip across the table — "between the Two Sisters to the sea." Tutu's imaginary boundary ran off the table's edge.

"Who gets the other half?" Darby's mind spun with confusion.

"Babette, your aunt Babe, as she'd want you to call her," Tutu said, "is on one side, and my son, Jonah, is on the other." Tutu drank off the cold tea in her cup, then smiled at Darby. "I'll bet he's wearing you out."

"Oh, no . . . ," Darby fibbed politely.

"Age has not turned Jonah into a gentleman."

"We're getting along okay now," Darby said. "But in the beginning, we didn't. At first, he made me feel more rebellious than my mother ever did, but at least he's not overly protective of me, like my mom."

"I doubt he'll leave you alone in the forest for long," Tutu told her. "He'd like a second chance at parenting, I think."

"So he adopted Cade," Darby said.

"He rescued Cade," Tutu corrected, as if Darby should see the difference.

Just then, a rustling sound came from nearby. Tutu was busy and didn't seem to notice, so Darby leaned back in her chair and took a quick look around.

In the dimmest corner of the cottage, something moved.

Darby blinked and then recoiled with a gasp.

An owl was balanced on a wooden perch, blissfully chewing the head off a mouse.

Darby bolted out of her chair, knocking it over behind her at the sight of the owl devouring its victim.

The owl opened its yellow eyes and glared at her.

"You know better!" Tutu scolded, and it took Darby a second to realize her great-grandmother was speaking to the owl. "He's supposed to eat outside," she said, aside, to Darby. "I don't know how he slipped that mouse past me."

The owl's head swiveled, looking anywhere but at the humans, until Tutu held the door wide and pointed at it. The owl gulped, made two quick grooming movements—one with his beak, the other with a claw—then swooped across the room.

Wind made by his flapping disturbed a carved walking stick that had been propped against the wall. It slammed to the cottage floor and the owl detoured away from the sound, skimming so near Darby's face that she heard air sing through its feathers. It banked left, fit its wide wings through the doorway, and was gone.

"Wow." Darby wished Heather, her best friend from home, were here. She would have loved the surprise of it. Wild owls didn't show up in Pacific Pinnacles. And they sure didn't bring along a takeout rodent to eat in a corner of your living room.

But then Darby reminded herself that not everyone had their family roots in old Hawaii. Owls were the *'aumakua*—a sort of guardian or reincarnated ancestor—of her family.

"I know *pueo* is our family guardian, but is that one a pet?" Darby asked.

Tutu tsked her tongue, then said, "More of a burglar."

Darby shivered, noticing the sky outside had gone cloudy. "I should probably get going. I've got a map, but I'm not too sure how far it is to the corral."

"I am," Tutu said. "You're very close, and I'll help you on your way."

"That would be wonderful," Darby said, and her spirits soared at the security of having a guide.

"I'll finish making lunch while you send Navigator home," Tutu said.

As quickly as her mood had soared, it plummeted.

Once she sent Navigator back to the ranch, she'd be a pedestrian again. Plus, she'd miss the brown gelding's sureness in finding his way home. But she'd promised to send him off when she got where she was going. If she didn't do it soon, Jonah would worry and come after her.

Hoku watched Darby emerge onto the cottage porch. Sorrel ears pointed at the girl as she balanced on one foot, then the other, tugging on her boots.

"Really fascinating, huh?" Darby teased her horse.

Hoku shook her head, then lowered her lips to the grass. The reins that were looped over Navigator's saddle horn barely allowed her to graze.

"How am I going to eat and keep hold of you at the same time?" Darby asked the filly, but it was Tutu who answered.

"Wait a bit more to send Navigator home. We'll sit on the step and watch them while we eat."

With none of the stiffness Darby expected from someone so old, Tutu sat on the wooden step, holding a plate of food. "Please help yourself," she said graciously.

First, Darby settled beside her great-grandmother and took a deep breath. She smelled ginger and sweet fruit, and her lungs expanded without a twinge.

"That tea was amazing," she said politely.

Then Darby picked up one of the smooth, white dumplings Tutu called a pork bun. Even though she was a pretty adventurous eater, Darby started with a slice of mango before taking a polite nip of the unfamiliar pork bun.

"Oh my gosh, you made this?"

The half-sweet, half-savory bun was delicious.

"It's nothing. You just put barbecued pork in a sweetened dough, roll it up like a ball, and cook it over steam." Tutu smiled as Darby popped the rest of the bun into her mouth. "You can get them in any Chinese restaurant in Los Angeles, I'm sure."

"Maybe," Darby said, "but I've never had one. Or two."

Darby ate more mango before reaching for another pork bun. Then she stopped snacking. She didn't want to waddle all the way to the *kipuka* corral.

"Ready to go?" Tutu asked after she'd returned the plate to the house. One hand covered the top of her walking stick. Her shapeless dress and scarf ends floated on wind Darby couldn't feel as Tutu took strong strides toward her.

"Sure," Darby said, then began talking to Hoku. "My favorite mustang," she smooched as Hoku nickered.

Only Hoku's eyes moved as she tracked Darby, lifting Navigator's reins over his head, then unhooked the loop of Hoku's lead rope from his saddle horn.

Navigator swallowed his last mouthful of grass and trotted off before Darby could swat him on the rump as Jonah had told her to do.

"Let's go," Tutu said, not giving Darby time to cast a melancholy look after the gelding.

They'd been walking only a few minutes when Darby heard something following them.

"That's Prettypaint," Tutu said, but the horse was gone before Darby saw her.

"Is she a pinto?" Darby asked.

"No, I've never known what color to call her, or which breed she is. She came to me as a pale gray with blue-gray spots on her heels, and your mother named her Prettypaint.

"She never wanders far, in case I want to ride, but she seems to know when I want to walk. I think she notices my stick," Tutu said, giving the ground a thump with her staff.

Darby was trying to do a quick calculation of her great-grandmother's age—her mom, Ellen, was thirty-five, so Jonah had to be at least fifty-five—when Tutu interrupted her thoughts.

"What? Are you surprised that an old lady like me still rides?"

"Not really," Darby said, thinking that Tutu must be over seventy-five years old, "but I think it's cool that you do. Not many ladies your age—whatever that is—are equestrians."

Tutu's laugh made Hoku turn with pricked ears.

"Hello, sweetheart." Tutu offered her palm for the filly to sniff, then whispered to Hoku, "Tell your girl that a woman raised on the Island of Wild Horses would be a sorry soul if she didn't learn to ride early and well."

Hoku glanced at Darby for permission, then extended her nose. Taking a noisy breath, the sorrel inhaled Tutu's scent, then allowed the old woman to stroke her mane.

That's how I want to be when I'm old, Darby thought. *Exactly.*

As they walked, Tutu told Darby that everything had come to Hawaii by wind, water, or wing.

"A seed could be blown here from another island, or washed up ashore or carried in the feathers of a bird," Tutu said. "But it took so very long for meat and plant eaters to arrive, most of our native plants and animals are defenseless."

"What do you mean?"

"Our briars don't have thorns. Our stinging nettles don't, either, and neither do our raspberries. Even the mint plants—which most animals shy away from—don't taste like mint. When pigs and chickens landed here, native plants served themselves up like a salad bar."

Darby frowned. She'd never thought of plants protecting themselves. Still, she'd bet poison oak would get trampled a lot more often if people weren't afraid of breaking out in an itchy rash.

"And the poor birds." Tutu shook her head. "They lived here so long without predators, they became flightless. When explorers from other islands arrived, all they had to do was walk up and club birds over the head."

Darby winced.

All at once, Hoku stopped. The white star on her chest rose as she breathed deeply and turned her head from side to side, nostrils flared.

"I don't see anything," Darby told the filly, but Hoku wasn't comforted.

"The rain forest is a good place to use senses other than your eyes," Tutu said. "You can't see more than a few yards in each direction anyway, since the trees stand so close to one another."

"I'm not sure my other senses are much good," Darby said.

"They are," Tutu said. "You've already learned to question what you think you know. You're open to other languages, like that of your horse. That's what being a horse charmer is about, yes?"

"I'm not sure I'm really a horse charmer like Jonah," Darby said, ducking her head. Even though her grandfather had said much the same thing to her this morning, she still didn't trust her mana enough to accept Tutu's praise.

Darby pulled gently on the lead rope, but Hoku still wouldn't follow.

"You have more confidence in my horse charming

than Hoku does," Darby complained, but quietly, so that she might pick up what the filly's swiveling ears heard.

"Here's where I leave you," Tutu said, giving Darby a hug. "Which way does your map take you from here?"

Darby slid the map out of her pocket. "From here," she said, turning the map so that the inverted *V* symbolizing Tutu's house was behind her, "I go past Pele's Porch?"

"It's just a hillside," Tutu clarified.

"And the Steam Vent?" Darby raised her eyebrows.

"Just what it sounds like," Tutu told her.

"And then over to the camp."

"Easy enough," Tutu said, "if you keep going downhill toward the sound of water."

Tutu's thin arms wrapped Darby in a hug that smelled of cookies and violets. Then she stepped back. "Don't forget, I'm only fifteen minutes away if you need me."

"I won't forget," Darby said, and then an exhilaration of being on her own sparked through her, and Darby led Hoku away.

A little while later, Darby noticed a notch in the hillside and decided that must be Pele's Porch. It was a good place to stop and scope out the place where she and Hoku would be camping. That way, she could see what she was walking into.

When she paused there, she had a view of the *kipuka* below.

The lush, primeval wood could have existed forever, wreathed by lava that stuck up like broken crystals around a forest of yellow and red flowered trees. Right in the center, almost like a bull's-eye, was the spot where she'd sleep tonight.

A bull's-eye? How ominous was that?

This is Hawaii, Darby lectured herself. *There's nothing to be afraid of down there.*

But she was taking no chances. She was in charge. If she led Hoku into danger, she'd have no one to blame except herself.

Okay, so the rain forest looked as if there was no threat in it.

Darby closed her eyes. There was no one around to make fun of her if she used her other senses the way Tutu had told her to do.

Darby sniffed. At first she caught nothing but the lush smell of green plants. Then, there was a dry, Halloweenish smell of brown leaves, and a moist smell like a shower that had misted up a mirror. Closer, she breathed in the sweet, leathery scent of Hoku.

Darby listened. Rainwater gushed gurgling over stones. A bird said, *E e vee.*

"I'm not like a snake," Darby told Hoku. "I can't flick out my forked tongue and taste danger." She didn't see, hear, smell, or taste anything wrong, Darby thought, so that left —

"Ow!" She gasped as Hoku lunged forward and stepped on the toe of her boot.

At the same time, she heard something crash through low branches in the rain forest below.

She held a finger to her lips for quiet, and made a quick, fruitless survey of what lay below, before trying to jerk her boot's toe out from under Hoku's hoof.

Her foot was trapped, but luckily Megan's hand-me-down boots were a little too big. Most of Hoku's weight rested on empty leather.

Darby pushed her palm against the filly's shoulder.

"Hoku, get off. Why do you pick *now* not to shy when I touch you?"

But the wild filly's attention was fixed on something in the rain forest.

For a creature that looked so weightless in motion, Hoku's single hoof was heavy. Darby imagined herself with cracked toe bones, limping to her destination.

"That's not going to happen," Darby told the filly.

Darby wrapped the striped lead rope around her hand, then leaned her shoulder against the filly's. She pushed with all her weight until finally, looking insulted, Hoku stepped away.

Darby would have grabbed her crushed foot and

groaned in relief if Hoku hadn't slipped past her, stalking whatever she'd sensed ahead.

"Is this it?" Darby asked. The unexpected sight transfixed her, too.

Steam came wavering up through a crack in the bottom of an indentation. She didn't know what it was called, but it looked like someone had dropped something big and heavy—like a truck—on the ground.

It was like something she'd see on the Discovery Channel, Darby marveled. Logically, it had something to do with volcanoes, but the Two Sisters were far off on the horizon.

Darby veered around it, and kept going downhill toward the rushing of water. Once the ground leveled out, Darby kept Hoku from eating some yellow flowers Auntie Cathy called Madagascar daisies, and then led the filly over hardened black lava.

Some of the lava had cooled in waves, but most of it had broken into shards. Still, Hoku picked her way over it, following Darby, as if she trusted her.

Then, there were trees crowded side by side, with branches poking out from ground level, instead of up on the trunk like Darby would have expected. And, finally, a clearing.

Someone had cut back trees growing around the corral and wooden lean-to, and the flat patch was overrun with grass, vines, and creeping plants.

Darby heard a splash. Her gaze followed the trail

of longer, greener grass. It showed where water pooled, became a rivulet, and wandered, losing its sense of direction, then going off on a tangent before it gathered enough water to become a real stream.

Head bobbing up and down, mane flowing in the waves, Hoku pulled Darby along.

At last, almost by accident, they both saw the place where the trickling water turned into a silvery moss brook, and a creature that almost had to be a mythical beast.

Not a unicorn. There was no such thing. But Darby decided it was a creature just as rare.

Drinking with her muzzle thrust into her rosy reflection, a pink horse stood.

 Chapter 4

Darby placed her hand over Hoku's nose, forming a grip of gentle dominance so the filly would stay quiet. Without looking, she knew the filly was about to greet the strange horse. She'd heard Hoku's lips move in the beginning of a nicker.

Puzzled by her human's use of horse sign language, Hoku lowered her head a little, but still watched the pink horse.

They both had a pretty good view, though the horse was about a quarter-mile downhill, in the center of the forest.

As the horse raised her head from drinking and backed away from the water, Darby saw she had large, wide-set eyes that suited her dished, Arab head. But her resemblance to an Arabian ended there.

The mare's black tail was low-set. Her black-maned neck wasn't high flung. Though she wasn't tall, her hooves looked nearly as big as Navigator's.

A different kind of beautiful from you, Darby thought. Her fingers tousled Hoku's mane as the filly nudged her knee, trying to pull Darby's attention away from the strange horse.

Sturdy and intelligent looking, the mare would be a horse you could count on in rough country. Or going over slick rocks near waterfalls.

Could she be a wild horse from Crimson Vale?

If she was, why had she wandered to a campsite with a corral and lean-to that must smell strongly of humans?

The mare had come for the water, of course. Jonah had said the stream ran pure and sweet. But the horse didn't take quick sips, then glance around warily as you'd expect a mustang to do.

She could be feral—once owned, then free—as Hoku had been.

Darby tried to think like a horse, but she didn't have much luck. She was too busy wondering if Manny, Cade's cruel stepfather, had managed to drive the entire wild herd from Crimson Vale. If the horses had split up, this could be one of them.

Or maybe the mare had wandered off on her own. Darby had read that wild stallions drove their male offspring away to live in little herds called bachelor bands. Could this mare have left with her girlfriends to explore the island?

Darby was thinking so hard, she wasn't ready for Hoku's whinny.

The pink mare looked right at them and trembled. When Hoku lifted her front hooves from the ground and gave a bad-tempered neigh, the roan backed through a thin spot in the foliage, which closed over the place where she'd been.

Darby released a sigh.

"Thanks, Miss Cranky Mouth," Darby said.

Hoku's unapologetic snort made Darby rub the sorrel's withers. She didn't have to be a horse charmer to understand that.

I'm not supposed to be petting you for no reason, Darby thought, but jealousy translated easily in any language. She wanted Hoku to know she had nothing to worry about.

All at once, Hoku's expression changed. She stepped forward, nostrils quivering with a longing that Darby recognized right away. As clearly as if she'd spelled it in the dirt with her hoof, Hoku had said "hay."

Darby sighed at her mistake.

Cade must have left some down there in the corral or lean-to. The filly loved hay above all other foods.

"So you weren't jealously guarding me," Darby said, but Hoku was in no mood to be teased. She stared at the lean-to, refusing to turn her head at Darby's tug on the lead rope. "You were worried that horse would get your hay, weren't you? Well, we have a way to go before we get to it."

They had to trek downhill, cross the lava rock, and walk through the rain forest before they reached the campsite.

You can't miss it, Cade had told her, but Darby still wanted to get going. If they hurried, they could get there before the sun set.

Just then, Darby spotted the perfect shortcut. A log had fallen in the rain forest and spanned the lava rock underneath. *Not quite perfect,* Darby realized as she took a closer look. It might be wide enough for Hoku to walk across, but the log was coated with moss. One misstep would send them both plummeting to the sharp lava rock below.

"C'mon, girl," Darby said, and Hoku must have understood her urgency, because she obeyed at once.

As soon as she and Hoku began picking their way down the hillside, they lost their overhead view of the campsite. At ground level, the trees formed a brown-and-green hump before them on the other side of the black lava rock.

Placing their steps carefully, they didn't make a single slip. Once they'd crossed the hard surface, Darby decided to pick up the pace.

It wouldn't be long before the sun sunk too low to penetrate the canopy of leaves.

"Let's hurry," she told her horse, but Hoku tossed her head, eyeing the wall of trees warily. Then the filly stopped.

Darby stroked Hoku's sweaty neck and looked at the forest as she would if she, like Hoku, had lived most of her life in Nevada. Even when Shan Stonerow had held her captive, the filly had been able to see open rangeland.

"I don't blame you, girl," Darby said.

Hoku had been in the forest before, but it had been with Navigator and the young geldings, so she'd felt the safety of a herd.

And sure, she and Hoku had walked through a forest in darkness, but it had been at the end of a day of fighting the sea and trotting over beach. Hoku had to have been as dazed as Darby was by the strangeness of their island initiation.

But she wasn't dazed now.

Twilight hung lavender in the sky, but there was still enough light for Hoku to know she shouldn't enter a place where she'd be surrounded. A prey animal wouldn't willingly walk into a trap.

Darby considered the forest through Hoku's eyes. There was nothing to her right or left but trees. Together, Darby and the filly looked over their shoulders.

Behind them, open space looked far away. Its brightness shrank with each step they took.

Overhead, there was a ceiling of leaves, branches,

and suddenly quiet birds, but no sky.

Chills prickled down Darby's arms. As soon as they were encircled by trees, Hoku would expect trouble.

And Darby was pretty sure she wasn't up to leading a paranoid horse.

"We have to use our other senses, like Tutu said." Darby tried to sound sympathetic.

Hoku didn't care what Tutu had said. She kept her hooves planted in place.

"When did you start balking?" Darby asked. Then, thinking her voice sounded too loud for the forest, she whispered, "This is Wild Horse Island, girl!"

Hoku wouldn't even look at her, until she tried to say the name in Hawaiian: "Moku Lio Hihiu."

Hoku's muzzle swung toward her so quickly, Darby had to duck out of her way.

"Moe-coo Lee-oh He-he-oo," she repeated, pretty sure she was pronouncing it right.

Of course horses couldn't skip, but Hoku made a skipping movement of delight just the same.

"Moe-coo Lee-oh He-he-oo," Darby said again, and when she continued walking, Hoku followed her.

The ground crunched. Hoku sniffed the forest floor, which was littered with round, penny-colored leaves. When the filly tried to nibble some purplish-black berries that were so shiny Darby could see the sorrel reflected in them, Darby pulled her away.

Even if Hawaiian plants had lost their poison and prickles, Darby wasn't sure they were safe for horses.

To distract the filly, Darby took a noisy breath, swelling out her chest, then exhaled just as loudly.

"I smell hay," she told her horse. "Don't you?"

Hoku's ears pricked up. Her eyes widened. Jogging, she towed Darby into the rain forest, to their temporary home.

Ferns grazed Darby's shoulders as she ducked to look into the wooden shelter. A sleeping bag, supplies, and hay were stacked inside a lean-to made of flat boards. They met at the top to make a triangular hut about four feet tall.

"I dub you the House of Ferns," Darby said melodramatically, but Hoku wasn't interested. The filly was thirsty, and once she saw that no other horse was munching her hay, Hoku tugged Darby toward the stream.

Even if Tutu hadn't told her the camp was rarely used, Darby would have known. Only a few hoofprints marked the damp dirt around the stream. She guessed they'd been stamped there by the roan, Cade's Appaloosa Joker, and some smaller animal with split hooves.

Maybe a fawn, she thought, smiling.

Holding the lead rope tightly, Darby knelt a few feet upstream from her horse. Once they'd finished drinking, Darby stood up to watch Hoku.

The filly surveyed this new place. Darby could

tell Hoku felt better with a little open space around her, but the filly's ears flashed in all directions, then pointed toward the corral.

Despite the comforting aroma of hay, Hoku didn't like the look of those fences.

"Hey, Hoku girl, let's see if I can lead you, carry hay, and open that gate, all at the same time," Darby said.

It didn't seem likely, so Darby decided to put Hoku in the corral first. Darby fumbled with the gate's lock, trying to peel off the tendrils of morning-glory vines that held it closed. Once the gate opened, Hoku shied, almost jerking the rope from Darby's hand.

"No problem, beauty," Darby said. With dusk closing in, she couldn't take the chance that the filly would break away. "Let's go get some food first."

Once they were close enough, Hoku nosed Darby out of the way, trying to grab a mouthful of hay.

"Don't be rude," Darby ordered the filly. Hoku blinked as if she had no idea what Darby was talking about, but she let Darby grab a flake of hay and hold it against her chest.

Sweet rumbling came from the filly as they returned to the corral. She walked fast now that she knew the hay was hers. Standing on tiptoe, Darby thrust the flake up, balanced it for a second on the top rail, and blinked against the hay dust sifting into her eyes, then tipped it over and inside the corral.

Hoku lowered her head, flattened her cheek to the ground, and slid her nose under the bottom rail. Darby laughed as the filly extended her tongue, tried to catch a stem of hay, and failed.

"Ready to go inside for some dinner?" Darby asked. Sighing, the sorrel followed Darby into the corral.

"Good girl," Darby said. She unclipped the lead rope to let the filly eat.

While Hoku ate, Darby returned to the lean-to and made the most of the remaining daylight. First, she shook out her sleeping bag, just as Megan had suggested. Next, she pumped fuel into a lantern as Jonah had taught her. Once she had the lantern glowing in the twilight, Darby sorted through the food Auntie Cathy had packed.

Since Darby hadn't trusted herself to use a camp stove—she had visions of burning down the forest— most of her food was snack stuff. Besides the fresh ham and cheese sandwich for dinner, there were six coconut cookies, a big packet of jerky, a smaller one of macadamia nuts, crunchy granola, three apples, a freeze-dried fruit-and-cinnamon-crumb mixture called Peach Pie Pak, and envelopes of powdered drink mix that she'd add to water.

Under it all, she found a huge bar of milk chocolate. The slab of candy was as thick as her hand and about twice as long.

"Oh, yeah. Thank you, Auntie Cathy," Darby

said, but she decided to save the candy for an emergency boost of energy, and hid it from herself.

"I'm set," Darby said with a nod.

Even though she was sure Auntie Cathy would send more food with the first person who came to check on her, she felt prepared to stay here alone. In fact, looking around the clearing, Darby felt a little territorial.

For company, she had Hoku and that other horse. Tutu was only fifteen minutes away. Maybe less, if she crossed on that log over the lava field.

Darby felt almost at home. She could live off her few provisions and never miss the company of other people.

Before she started thinking like her great-grandmother, Darby decided she wouldn't mind a visit from Megan, or Heather. Or Samantha Forster.

"Yes!" Darby said, and Hoku's head jerked up. "It's okay, girl."

She'd love for the Nevada cowgirl to see that the Phantom's sister wasn't the frightened, desperate horse she'd been in the winter.

Right now, for instance, Hoku was sniffing around for a last bit of dinner. Sam wouldn't be surprised at proof of the mustang's ability to adapt, but Darby would bet she'd be proud.

Darby crawled into her sleeping bag and turned off the lantern. Blackness surrounded her, but she immediately blotted out all forest sounds with a yawn. Her hours of riding and hiking caught up with her, and she fell asleep.

In her dream, Darby sat on the Sun House lanai, telling her mother of her Hawaiian adventures. As she did, a voice boomed out like a movie ad for coming attractions, saying, "Season of the cave spider!"

Darby woke kicking. She tried to pull her legs clear of the sleeping bag, but only managed to hit her knees against her chin before rolling out of the lean-to and knocking the lantern over.

"Fire," she gasped, but she'd turned off the lantern before she'd fallen asleep. And she couldn't have dozed for more than a few minutes, because the lantern's wick hadn't lost all of its glow.

Darby wiggled free of her sleeping bag, then stood and listened.

What had wakened her?

Not Hoku. Darby could just pick out her filly's silhouette by the glint of her eyes. The mustang watched her, but she didn't seem agitated.

Branches creaked in a warm wind.

The spilled lantern fuel smelled like gasoline.

Leaves crunched and pricked her heels. Darby could not believe she'd gone to sleep barefoot.

Maybe her brain had been trying to remind her of happy-face spiders or cane spiders or tarantulas—did Hawaii have tarantulas?—because she'd heard of a dance called the tarantella that people did to flush out tarantula venom, and the way she was hopping around now, trying to tug her socks back on so that nothing crawled between her toes and bit her, she was probably doing it!

Mud. Darby held her breath at the sound of something walking in mud.

With her second sock safely stretched to her shin, she eased her foot down so that she wouldn't tip over, and concentrated.

A squishy sound, like a foot pulling free of mud, came to her ears again.

Please, not Manny, she thought, but nothing as big as Cade's creepy stepfather could move that way. She remembered the reek of perspiration coming from his tattooed and sweaty torso. Not only would she be able to smell him, Hoku would, too.

Darby heard no underlying plunk, like a horse hoof, splashing in the stream. And if it had been a horse, Hoku would have greeted it. Or warned it away from her hay.

No, the creature sounded too aimless. Equines didn't blunder around, between the stream and stream bank.

A sucking sound reminded Darby of the third set of tracks beside the water. Smaller tracks, and she'd thought it was marks from a fawn.

A fawn!

How dumb are you? Darby asked herself. *Have you seen a single deer on this island?*

What else had cloven feet and moved around the forest in the dark?

Darby heard quarrelsome grunting, and suddenly she knew.

Chapter 5

If you think you hear one, you do.

That's what Jonah had said about wild pigs. He'd also told her they gobbled down birds and rooted trenches that she could trip over.

Darby took a deep breath.

Calm down and think, she told herself.

But she couldn't help wondering how pigs did that rooting. Her curiosity wasn't the usual Discovery Channel variety, either. She pictured medieval tapestries with wild boars goring hounds and horses.

They couldn't do that ripping with their snouts. They had tusks.

She bet Hawaiian pigs had tusks, too. If so, how

long were they? Why hadn't she asked more questions when Kit, Auntie Cathy, Jonah, Megan, Cade, and, shoot, *everyone* around her had warned her about pigs?

Still listening to the muddy meandering, Darby wondered why this pig didn't move more stealthily. It was wild, or at least feral—a tame animal that lived free. It must have scented her and Hoku.

She stared into the darkness, wishing for just a pinch of Cade's famous night vision.

She shook her head slowly, trying to figure out why the creature didn't care if she heard it. Finally, Darby guessed it was possible that the wild pigs had no predators except for humans, and maybe this animal had sized her up as no threat.

It still didn't seem right.

At last, the squelchy steps moved away. Leaves rustled, then the quiet night pressed in around her once more.

Darby longed for daylight. She wouldn't fall back asleep, and she wanted to write down her questions about the pig.

Not that it had to be a pig. She didn't really know what was out there in the dark, but she'd figure it out on her own. Otherwise, Jonah might make her return to the ranch before her time alone with Hoku was over.

E e vee. E e vee.

Darby awoke outside of her shelter. Curled up on

one side, atop her sleeping bag, she yawned. Then she rolled onto her back and opened her eyes.

Nice bedroom ceiling, she thought, taking in the interlaced branches and leaves overhead.

A red bird bobbed next to a red flower in a treetop. The bird and flower matched exactly.

A wavy branch returned to the very base of the trunk instead of sprouting from a bigger branch. The branch next to it did the same thing, gliding up to point out the royal blue sky.

In April, it was as warm as summer.

Impatient hooves tapped the earth and Hoku nickered.

"I'll be right there," she almost sang to her horse.

Darby pointed her toes and stretched her ground-cramped legs.

It was Tuesday, but she had hours of freedom with her horse. Next week at this time, she'd be in school. Confined to a classroom.

Urgency replaced Darby's dreaminess. She bolted to her feet and started getting dressed.

As she slipped off her jeans and replaced them with shorts, Darby checked her skin for spider bites.

Not one! So much for Cade's warnings.

She slid her feet into tennis shoes and pulled the laces tight.

Her feet felt so light without boots that Darby skipped as she led Hoku to water.

Wavy marks showed where the stream had risen

during the night, then receded. *It must be fed by the ocean and respond to the tides,* she thought, trying not to care that pig tracks the size of her palm were imprinted on the damp dirt. Hoku sniffed them, flattened her ears, and snorted, as if blowing the scent from her nostrils.

"You've never smelled a pig before!" Darby realized. "I'll have to write to Sam and ask her, but I've never heard of wild pigs living with wild horses in Nevada."

Darby tried to eat some granola before putting Hoku back in her corral, but the filly nudged at her hand and breathed in the smell of oats and honey.

"Hey, I want to *eat* my breakfast, not wear it," Darby told her horse. When Hoku pulled back, wide-eyed at the girl's sharp tone, Darby added, "You're cute, but I'll be training you to be a brat if I let you have it after you've been so pushy."

Fending off the filly's nose with her elbows, Darby ate a handful of granola before leading Hoku back to the corral.

There, she brushed Hoku all over, even her head, despite the filly's glare.

"I know you don't like me to touch your head," Darby sympathized.

She still couldn't imagine a man cruel enough to whip the young horse in the face, but Sam's fax had hinted that it was likely Shan Stonerow had done just that. Jonah and Cade agreed that was the story the filly's head-shyness told, too.

But Hoku was less fearful now. Darby could tell the filly wasn't afraid, just annoyed because Darby wouldn't do what she wanted, so Darby dusted the soft brush along Hoku's golden nose until the horse bared her teeth.

"Don't you do that!" she scolded the filly, then crowded in front of her and held both sides of her halter. "You know I'd never hurt you."

Hoku rolled her eyes until the whites showed, then looked away, trying to duck behind her forelock. But she didn't struggle or try to shake off Darby's grip. When Darby didn't move away, Hoku swished her tail as if she'd been misunderstood.

"Let's try it again," Darby said. She released her hold on the halter and began brushing Hoku's face again. This time, only the skin on Hoku's neck twitched.

"That's better, baby," she told her horse.

Jonah had told her to accustom Hoku to a variety of sounds and textures before trying her with a saddle blanket, so she tried rubbing the filly all over with a burlap grain sack Cade had stashed in the hut for just that purpose.

Hoku didn't resist the burlap's scratchiness. In fact, she leaned toward Darby's hand as if the rough texture felt good.

"How about this?" Darby asked, trailing a piece of plastic bubble wrap over her horse. At first Hoku jumped away, but then she nudged the thing.

Hoku found no danger in it, but when the beautiful sorrel let her ears sag to each side, Darby laughed.

Hoku clearly thought bubble wrap was a really dumb idea, and she wanted Darby to know she was only tolerating it because Darby had asked her to do it.

"Good girl. I think you're ready for a test," Darby said.

She offered Hoku a clump of feathers to sniff.

It was the remains of an orange feather boa. Megan said her dog Pip had "played with it to death," in protest over being left home alone.

Now, Hoku nosed the feathers, licked them, then shook her head.

"Well, you're not supposed to eat them," Darby said.

Hoku didn't like the feathers tickling her flank, but she only kicked out once, straight behind, to tell Darby.

A few seconds later, Darby dangled the feathers in front of Hoku, then drew them gently over the mustang's face.

Hoku's tongue thrust from her mouth as she watched Darby.

Hmm. Kit had told her to watch the filly for "mouthing." If she licked her lips, it meant she was giving in, like a foal to its mother. But Hoku wasn't licking, she was just trying to clean bits of fluff from her lips.

Finally, the horse sighed and her muscles looked looser, less tense.

That's trust, Darby thought.

"And it's good enough for me," she told Hoku.

Then she gave her horse a hug.

Darby's arms had just joined around Hoku's neck when a voice spoke from the forest.

"Make her into a pet, and you're going to be sorry."

Darby whirled toward the sound.

It had to be Jonah, but what was he doing here?

The filly didn't bolt or buck. Far less spooked than Darby, she simply sidestepped a few yards away.

"Pretty good," Darby told Hoku, trying to keep her voice from shaking. Then she marched over to the gate, leaving the corral to go tell Jonah what she thought of his surprise.

She would have, that is, if she knew where he was hiding.

The birds had stopped flitting around and calling, so they'd heard him, too, but that didn't help.

Too stubborn to ask where he was, Darby stood with her hands on her hips until Jonah said, "I don't want her to see me. Keep her focused on you."

She followed the voice and found her grandfather. He stood beside a stone so bearded with lichen, it looked like an old man.

Jonah seemed relieved that she'd made it through

the night and Darby longed to tell him about the owl in Tutu's cottage, the log over the gully, and the pig in the night, but all that came out was, "I'm not making Hoku into a pet."

"If she just stands around waiting for food like a poodle . . ."

Darby had nothing against poodles. She liked poodles. What she didn't like was Jonah's tone.

". . . it'll be harder on her in the long run. Unless" — Jonah paused as if musing — "you're going to keep her in a stall all the time. Then it won't matter."

Boarding Hoku in a stall in a Los Angeles stable would be a nightmare for the filly and everyone around her, Darby thought. Even if it was financially possible. Which it wasn't.

"But if she's going to live in an open pasture on the ranch, you don't want her to lose her fear."

"Wait." Darby grabbed her temples, as if she could squeeze understanding into her head. She let her hands drop when she realized she'd unconsciously copied one of Jonah's gestures. "I can see why I'd want her to be independent, but why would I want her to be afraid?"

"For the same reason you should be afraid of fire, traffic, things like that. They can hurt you. You can't train her to face every dangerous situation. It's not possible.

"Right now, Hoku has an advantage over domestic horses," Jonah went on. "She's been wild. She's had to think for herself, yeah? Let her keep her instincts."

"What does that have to do with hugging?" Darby asked.

Jonah gave her a look that was impatient, but not angry. "It's good that she trusts you, but if you give her attention for no reason, she may not listen when you need her to go against her instincts."

Darby resisted the urge to tell her grandfather that he made her head hurt. Instead, she blurted, "I met Tutu."

"Yeah?"

"I like her. She's so cool," Darby said.

"Cool," Jonah repeated with a smile.

"And she said I remind her of my mom," Darby told him, and in that instant, he was harder to read than a horse.

She saw flashes of surprise, irritation, and regret cross his face before he abruptly changed the subject.

"Do you know what they call that?" Jonah asked as a yellow bird darted past them and disappeared into the greenery.

"I didn't get a very good look, but a *honeycreeper*? Or did that bird have kind of a crossbeak?" Darby used her hands to show him what she thought she'd seen, a bird bill that she thought only existed in kids' picture books.

Jonah nodded, smiling. "They call it the Swiss Army knife of birds."

Darby laughed.

"It's true," Jonah said, and then, clearly pleased by her interest in her Hawaiian home, he pointed at a tall fern. "Feel this. Right here. Pretty soft, yeah?"

Jonah stroked a knuckle over the tightly curled center of the fern.

"It feels like velvet," she said, doing the same.

"These ferns grow near volcanoes. They were used to make shelters for those who came to worship Pele, the volcano goddess," Jonah explained.

"But we're a long way from a volcano, so—Oh! The steam vent?" Darby asked, pointing back the way she and Hoku had entered the forest.

"Maybe, or maybe the pig-fish man just liked it here."

"The pig-fish man?" Darby echoed. For one spinning second, she remembered those grunting, slippery sounds in the night.

"He was a shape-shifter in love with Pele," Jonah said in the same offhand way he might say the guy was a plumber. "She got tired of him following her around and turned him into this fern." Jonah nodded at her hand. "Soft as a pig's snout, yeah?"

"I don't know," she grumbled, but suddenly the fern felt hairy, not silky. She crossed her arms and tucked her fingers inside her fists.

Each time she had a conversation like this—about

Pele, family guardians, or *menehune*, the island's little people — Darby felt confused. She wanted to honor her Hawaiian ancestors. Surprisingly, she really felt a bond with them. But did that mean she had to believe these stories?

It's all about mana, she told herself. Some things she learned and others she felt, and she did not feel like believing in the pig-fish man.

"Don't worry," Jonah said. He rubbed the pad of his thumb between her eyebrows, and Darby figured she must have been frowning. "The pig-fish man doesn't hold a grudge. Each year, the first frond from this fern is red."

"For Pele?" Darby guessed, thinking red might be the favorite color of a volcano goddess.

"Yes," Jonah said. "So, everything go okay last night?"

Darby drew a deep breath. If she told him about the midnight intruder, he'd tease her about the pig-fish man. If she told him about the pink horse, he'd have a story for that, too.

"Everything was fine," Darby said at last. "Hoku ate one and a half flakes of hay, and I ate my sandwich and a third of my cookie stash."

Jonah's brown eyes studied Darby.

Was she imagining that nerves had given her voice a higher pitch?

"That reminds me," he said. "It was Megan's turn to make dinner last night, and she made something she's calling paniolo pizza. No such thing, if you ask me. More like an inside-out pizza. She sent you one." Jonah handed Darby a foil packet. "It's good, but cold now."

"Cold pizza is one of my favorite things," Darby said. "My mom and I used to have it for breakfast sometimes."

"Do you think she'll—" As if the words had burned his tongue, Jonah sucked in a breath. "Don't matter. Something's wrong with the water heater in the bunk house. Go gossip with your horse." He lifted his chin toward the corral. "She has time for it. I don't."

He turned to go and Darby, despite her confusion, heard shifting hooves and knew Jonah had tied Kona where Hoku wouldn't see him.

"You don't forget, though," Jonah said, not turning around. "If you let that filly keep a few of her instincts, she'll live longer."

He made sense, Darby thought as she began walking back toward the corral and Hoku, but sometimes she had trouble putting his advice into action.

She must have been concentrating on his steps moving away, because suddenly Darby heard Jonah make an expression of surprise, and she stopped.

Darby's lips were pursed to say his name, when she recognized a voice she didn't expect to hear.

"Son," Tutu greeted Jonah.

Why would a note of reprimand be mixed with Tutu's glad tone? Probably it wasn't, Darby thought, but when Jonah responded "Mother," and moments of silence followed, Darby wished she could see their faces.

At last Jonah cleared his throat and said, "I'm not interfering. Just bringing her food."

Darby jumped in surprise. She had to be the "her" Jonah was talking about.

"I thought that was Cade's job," Tutu said.

"He had other work," Jonah said, and Darby felt suspicious all over again.

If Cade had done something that contributed to Ben Kato's death, he wouldn't like returning to the clearing.

"She knows how to work with horses," Tutu said, and Darby heard pride in her great-grandmother's voice.

"She's coming along," Jonah admitted.

And that, Darby told herself, was the perfect time to creep away. But her feet stayed still.

She looked down at them and caught her breath. Jonah had mentioned how small rain-forest spiders were, and he was right.

A tiny spider leg—so small, she wouldn't have seen it if she hadn't been focused on her feet—trembled to get a grip on the toe of Darby's white sneaker.

"Are you saying I have nothing to offer her?" Jonah asked.

Darby listened, watching the brave little spider climb the Himalaya of her shoe.

Finally, the spider was up. It rested before tackling the hills of her shoelaces and she saw the minuscule white markings that made the spider have a "happy face."

"You always told me, 'without the trunk there are no branches,'" Jonah pointed out.

The saying made Darby look up and smile.

That Hawaiian proverb was pretty easy to understand, and a lot nicer way to train kids to respect their elders than some she'd heard.

"Ohia branches spring from the same root as the tree," Tutu said.

I saw those, Darby thought, wondering if the trees she'd been studying when half awake that morning were the ones Tutu was talking about.

"But the trunk has been around longer," Jonah joked.

What is this, dueling proverbs? Darby wondered, but now that Tutu and Jonah were both laughing, she remembered to look back down at the spider. It had almost reached her bare ankle.

I admire your determination, Darby thought, *but you're not crawling on my skin.*

Darby lifted her foot and gave it a gentle shake.

With the willpower of a pit bull, the spider held on.

Darby shivered, but she couldn't dance around to dislodge the spider, while she was eavesdropping.

Get off! she commanded silently, then planted the

heel of her shoe and jiggled the toe back and forth. She realized her mistake when the spider lost its grip and landed on her shin.

Darby squinched her eyes closed and jerked the neck of her T-shirt up to cover her mouth against a silent scream.

You're just a little spider.

You don't bite.

I'm not afraid of you.

Some distance off, Kona snorted and saddle leather creaked. Jonah must be mounting his horse to ride back to the ranch.

Good. Then she could get rid of this tiny trespasser.

But Jonah didn't move off before Tutu had the last word.

"It will be better for all of us if you don't forget another of my favorite sayings, which you brushed aside while you were raising her mother."

Her mother. Darby really wanted to hear this.

"What's that?" Jonah sighed as if Tutu was picking on him.

"Without subjects, there is no king."

Okay, she'd mull that over later, but she couldn't take time to make sense of it now, because Kona's hooves were thudding away and the thump of Tutu's walking stick followed.

At last, Darby bent down and grabbed a leaf. She held it against her shin.

"Crawl onto this," she whispered, offering the happy-face spider an alternate route to wherever it was going. "That's it. Yes!"

Careful not to drop the creature, Darby placed the leaf on the rain-forest floor. She exhaled, shook her arms crazily, as if spiders had been creeping all over her, then ran back to Hoku as fast as she could.

Chapter 6

Penny-shaped leaves puffed up from Darby's shoes as she jogged back to camp.

A little out of breath, she stood waiting, but no one came after her.

So Tutu wasn't coming to visit. Maybe she, like Jonah, had just been making sure her city slicker great-granddaughter had survived her first night in the rain forest. And, since Jonah had taken care of that, she'd returned home.

Overstuffed with all she'd heard, Darby's mind craved a simple task.

"I'll think about all that mother and son, father and daughter stuff later," Darby told Hoku as she passed the corral. "Now we're going to do something fun."

She dug into her backpack and pulled out the brown paper bag Megan had given her. Some kind of fun training tool, Megan had promised.

Darby sat back on her heels. It was a plastic jar of bubbles.

"Okay," she said to herself, then backed out of her hut and stood before unscrewing the lid.

She extracted the slippery pink wand and blew.

Three of four iridescent bubbles popped almost as soon as they formed, but one drifted away, rising on tropical breezes.

Hoku nickered, then bolted away from the bubble.

"You're safe, girl." Darby walked closer to the corral, drew a deep breath, and blew a long stream of bubbles.

Wide-eyed, Hoku launched a kick. When she turned her head to check on her pursuers, an aqua-pink bubble bumped her nose and burst.

Halfway into lowering her head for a buck, Hoku stopped. Her tongue wagged out to lick the bubbles' residue. She shook her forelock and shuddered.

"Not too tasty?" Darby asked.

She blew flocks of bubbles, including one as big as her head, before she dipped the wand, held her arm straight out, and spun in a circle, letting the breeze create a silvery school of bubbles, accustoming the wild filly to another strange thing.

When Hoku finally stopped noticing them, Darby

dropped the wand back in the jar and screwed the lid on.

"I'll be right back," she said, then returned to her hut to get her diary.

She wanted to write down what Jonah had told her about preserving Hoku's wild instincts. She should remember, but it had sounded like one of the mana lessons and it was a little confusing. Sometimes writing helped her sort out complicated ideas.

She had to write down the conversation between him and Tutu as well and make notes about the wild horse. In fact, she had a lot to think about, and there was no reason she couldn't do it inside Hoku's corral.

Darby knelt on her sleeping bag inside her house of ferns. She found her notebook and was about to crawl back outside, when she heard the breath of a winded horse.

Had someone ridden into her camp? Or was it the wild horse?

Darby flattened herself against her sleeping bag, keeping out of sight. The horse was riderless. With her coat sweat-drenched and shaded by the trees, she didn't look pink. She was the deep red of a gemstone whose name Darby couldn't quite recall.

From her ground-level position, she had a much closer view of the mare than she had yesterday from the steam-vent ridge. The mare was so still, she might have been carved from garnet.

That's it—garnet, Darby thought. The motionless

mare hardly seemed to breathe.

But then, looking alert but not afraid, the mare raised her head and searched the clearing. Her wet neck twisted from side to side and she ignored Hoku's nickers.

What are you looking for, girl? Darby wondered. Somewhere in her mind, she knew what, besides water, had drawn the mare here. She just hadn't figured it out yet, because she was fixated on the feud between Megan and Cade.

Deep-chested and broad-hooved, the mare's conformation was a match for the form of Black Lava, the stallion from Crimson Vale.

Except for her scars.

Darby winced at the slashes scoring the mare's stomach and hind legs. They cut through the horse's pink hair, down to her black hide.

Wild horses ran at the first sign of danger. So why had the mare stayed still long enough to be ripped that way?

Maybe she'd been protecting a foal. Or she might have fallen. A vine might have acted as a snare and some predator, seeing her apparently helpless, had attacked.

Before Darby reached a conclusion, the mare picked her way to the corral. She and Hoku touched noses, squealed, and shied. Their hooves clattered and tapped, but they moved only a few feet from each other, then returned to sniff each other's necks.

Lifting her chin as high as she could, Hoku looked past the roan to Darby. Hoku's look-at-me snort made the other horse turn.

A whorl of hair on the roan's forehead had the effect of making her look friendly. The mare spotted Darby and studied her.

Since she'd already been noticed, Darby crawled out of her hut and straightened, inch by inch, until she stood at her full height. The mare blinked. Muscles in her shoulders tensed, but Darby stood absolutely still.

The mare didn't bolt until Darby spoke.

"Tango—"

The first syllable of the name had barely left Darby's mouth when the roan recoiled and collided with the fence. Then, Tango backed away, head jerking skyward, still scrutinizing Darby.

She'd been expecting Megan, of course, because this was the rose roan, the pink horse Megan had lost on the day her father had died.

It made sense that the horse would mistake her for the other girl. Megan must have grown in the last eighteen months, but the mare remembered her as she had been.

Darby lifted her hand from her side and extended it toward the confused roan.

Tango was a tame horse. Or had been. So it shouldn't be that hard to lure her closer.

It's okay, she told the mare silently. *You're safe here.*

Someone, probably Megan's dad, judging by those scars, had ridden Tango on the day of the accident. Carrying a rider, the mare wouldn't have been able to flee when she sensed danger. Reins would have held her in place until the pain came and it was too late.

This time, nothing will hurt you.

The mare had bad memories of this place, but she'd returned.

If only I knew what drew you here, Darby thought, *maybe I could remind you what gentle human hands feel like, and give Megan a head start on winning you back.*

A slippery sound came from Hoku and Darby noticed the filly licking at her nose where the bubble had broken.

The bubbles! Of course. Megan had told her she'd used bubbles with Tango. She hadn't said Tango by name, of course; she'd just mentioned using them with her horse.

What if Tango had caught the bubble scent, so different from anything else in the rain forest, and sought out the kind human with the bubbles?

Still facing the horses, Darby bent her knees and reached behind her for the plastic bottle.

Hoku's rapt expression made Darby smile, but then she wobbled, knocking over her backpack. It hit the camp lantern and it struck the jar of bubbles, which rolled out of reach.

The noise was bad enough, but when Darby

swiveled to grab the jar, the mare jumped a full length away from the corral. With her second leap, she was gone and the rustle of leaves faded into silence.

Oh yeah, I'm some horse charmer, Darby thought. It was a good thing Jonah hadn't been here to see the mess she'd made of trying to trust her mana.

Hoku neighed after the mare. She paced along her fence, shot Darby a glare, then neighed again.

"I know, it was my fault this time," Darby confessed.

Jonah had talked about letting Hoku keep her instincts. This must be what he'd meant. Tango might have been drawn to the clearing by food and company, but her wild instincts told her not to take any chances with strange girls who made loud noises.

It was late afternoon when Cade showed up.

He emerged from the rain forest so silently, he was in the middle of Darby's camp before she noticed him.

Had he gotten over feeling guilty about this place where Ben died? Darby wondered. Or maybe he'd gotten over his sadness.

It wasn't like he was a suspect, Darby thought, but all the same it was relief that made Darby blurt out her news before Cade said a word.

"Megan's horse isn't dead. I found her. Well, saw her. At least, I'm pretty sure I did."

Cade went so still, he could have passed for one

of the rain-forest trees.

"A rose roan," Darby rushed on, "about fourteen hands high, with a little"—Darby pinwheeled her index finger on her forehead—"twirl in her hair, here."

Cade carried a rifle. Darby blinked, amazed she'd just noticed.

Everything about the young paniolo was meant to blend in. His pullover shirt was a shade between buff and faded green. His tanned face was a close match for his brown hat. His short, vaquero-style braided hair, which would have looked startlingly blond, was tucked up, out of sight.

His arms hung at his sides. He held a packet of something that smelled delicious and was undoubtedly for her in his right hand. But he gripped a rifle in his left.

"That horse skull wasn't hers," Cade muttered, and Darby had been so distracted, it took her a few seconds to remember the rumor of Cade's stepfather having a horse skull nailed up on a barn wall.

She thought of the tales of the Shining Stallion, too, a horse Jonah had reportedly shot, and Cade's comment didn't make much sense to her.

"Why would the skull be hers? Didn't it show a bullet hole?"

"Forget it." Cade gave his head a quick shake. "How long ago?" He pushed the food parcel at Darby. "I've got to go get her."

"Let's do it together," Darby said, and though she took the parcel, she ignored the aroma of chicken and sesame.

"I lost her; I'll catch her," Cade snapped.

"You lost her?" Darby asked. "Were you riding Tango?"

Cade looked right at Darby, but his eyes lost focus. She had the feeling he was reliving that day.

He looked almost bewildered. But just for an instant. Then his expression hardened and he said, "Megan wasn't riding Tango and neither was I. Ben was. . . ."

And Ben died.

"But I lost her."

With Cade standing right in front of her, Darby couldn't find the solution to the mystery. If Cade said he'd lost Tango, he probably had. But why had Ben died?

"Well, I saw Tango about three hours ago," Darby estimated. "So you might as well keep me company while I eat."

Cade started to refuse, but then he lowered himself to sit on the sleeping bag she'd dragged out of her hut so they didn't have to sit on the dirt.

"Is that why you didn't want to come out here?" Darby asked.

Cade frowned, then shook his head. "I was helping Kimo fix the idiot water heater."

"Oh," she said.

Darby didn't expect Cade to be a chatty dinner companion, and he wasn't, but she was too busy unwrapping the package of Auntie Cathy's spring rolls to interrogate him any further.

Her mouth watered with sudden hunger and when Cade motioned her to go ahead and eat, she did.

For a second, Darby considered unearthing the chocolate bar she'd hidden.

Feeling guilty and a little greedy, she didn't, but she did offer him her last coconut cookie—which he accepted—before she bit into her spring roll.

"Mmm," Darby said. "Thanks for bringing this."

Cade gave a half smile. He sat cross-legged with the rifle across his lap. Darby trusted him to be careful, but the weapon made her uneasy.

"Why didn't you leave that on your saddle?" she asked.

"In my scabbard," he corrected.

"Okay," Darby said, biting her lip for a second. "Or why didn't you just ride in here?"

"You're not supposed to ride in this forest. Jonah and your tutu don't allow it. And there's no way I'd leave my rifle unattended," he said. The way he stroked a hand over his polished wooden stock made Darby think he was proud of it, but he added, "Besides, what's the sense in carrying a rifle if it's out of reach?"

Did he mean Joker could spook and the rifle could fall? Or did he think he might need a gun?

Darby didn't ask, and Cade shifted the topic to her homework from Jonah. She was supposed to write down twenty-five things Hoku did tomorrow.

"Anything?" Darby asked. "Like scratching her neck on the fence?"

"Yeah," Cade said.

Darby thought about this as she chewed her spring roll and drank gulps of water. She could see the sense in Jonah's assignment. Observing Hoku's sounds and movements was something Darby did instinctively, but she'd probably think about them more carefully if she wrote them down.

With her stomach full, Darby noticed the thoughtful way Cade broke a piece off his cookie. He popped it into his mouth, but Darby didn't think he savored it.

He's still brooding over Tango, she thought, but then Cade began talking about something totally different.

"In the old days, when paniolo were just getting started, they'd find bulls in the forest. They were too wild to herd back to the ranch, so they'd rope 'em and tie 'em to a tame ox overnight. The calm creature soothed the rough one, yeah? And when a rider came back out in the morning, he could lead 'em both home."

Cade took a breath and looked at Darby to see if she understood.

What in the world did this have to do with Tango? Darby wondered, but she nodded, encouraging Cade to go on.

"Just for a little experiment, me and Ben tried that. . . ."

Darby felt chills, thinking Megan's dad must have been a kind man, to work with the abused boy Cade had been when Jonah first adopted him. In just a few words, Cade had implied that Ben had taught him paniolo ways and treated him like a partner.

"Ben was nice to you," Darby said.

"Ben was nice to everybody," Cade snapped, but he looked a little confused. "The only thing anyone could fault him for was being a little too thrifty."

"Thrifty?" Darby asked.

"Pani said when they were sharing the bunkhouse, before Ben married Cathy, the biggest fight they ever got in was Pani refusing to wash plastic wrap and reuse it."

Normally Darby would have laughed, but Cade didn't. He just swept his hat off and looked steadily at its woven crown.

Now that she had him talking, Darby wanted Cade to stop. She could tell the memories hurt him.

"Yeah," Cade said, finally. "Ben was nice to me, and yoking the cattle together worked better even than we figured. Other cattle had come crowdin' around here"—Cade gestured at the clearing—"waiting for us to bring 'em food.

"What happened is, we were taking 'em up, hadn't reached the lava rock yet, and there were pigs on the path. How could I not know that it's always open season on pigs?" Cade sighed. "Anyway, the cattle would have walked on by, but a piglet got separated from its family and started squealing. The sow answered. The boar charged Tango."

The sounds rang in Darby's imagination. Pigs squealing. Men shouting. A horse screaming.

"Tango was broke, but still green. Ben sweet-talked her in Hawaiian—sounded like singing—but the boar ran right between her front legs and she reared. She went over backward on Ben." Cade's hand fisted, turning the rest of his cookie into a shower of crumbs.

Darby sat motionless, waiting for Cade to go on. When he did, she had to lean forward to hear his voice.

"He told me to go after Tango." Cade looked over his shoulder as if watching his younger self gallop into the forest after the terrified mare. "Must've been fifteen, twenty minutes before it hit me. Something wasn't right."

Cade gave a dry laugh and slapped the stock of his rifle. "Yeah. *Something*. I came back and Ben'd already, you know, passed over."

Darby tried to see the scene with Megan's eyes. Cade left Ben Kato alone and dying. But Cade wasn't to blame, Darby thought.

Ben Kato had been a paniolo. He'd told Cade to go after Tango, and Darby could absolutely imagine Jonah, Kit, or Cade himself putting the welfare of his injured horse above his own.

Hoku pawed in her corral.

"Fed your horse lately?" Cade asked.

"Not lately enough, according to her," Darby said.

The joke was weak, but feeding Hoku would give Cade a few minutes alone. The dark red of his face said he needed them.

As she tossed hay to the delighted filly, Darby thought of Tango's scars. The rose roan had been gored under the belly and down her hind legs, but she'd survived. Tango must have learned lessons from her wild ancestors that had kept her alive, without human help.

"That's what Jonah wants for you," Darby whispered to Hoku, but the filly wasn't taking anything seriously except the stalks of hay, which bristled from each side of her mouth like huge cat whiskers.

Cade blamed himself for more than Tango's escape, Darby realized, and all of a sudden, the way Cade had looked on the night he'd come back from searching for Hoku made sense.

Cade's face had been dirty and maybe even tear streaked. He'd looked as if everything depended on him finding Hoku.

That night, Darby hadn't understood why he'd

run Joker too hard, risking his own horse to catch hers.

Now she got it. His determination to find the filly had had nothing to do with her and Hoku, but everything to do with the way he'd failed before.

But Darby knew he was wrong. He hadn't failed. There was nothing he could have done to save Ben, but she wasn't good at stuff like this, talking to people about problems, so when she walked back into camp, she asked, "If a horse rears when you're riding it, what are you supposed to do?"

"Get on its neck," Cade said slowly. "Put your weight forward."

He was sifting his words, trying not to say anything that might make Ben look bad.

"Is that what Ben did?"

Cade stared at the camp lantern as he pumped it up. It brightened his face, so he couldn't hide his hard-set, misshapen jaw.

"He was a paniolo. He did what was right."

"And you're a paniolo, too."

"Not like him," Cade said. He took one look at Darby's face, and stood to go.

"After a man is smashed by a horse, what could you do for him? What could he have done for you?" Darby blurted. It wasn't very tactful, but she had to get the words out before Cade left. "You said you were only gone for fifteen or twenty minutes. No one could have galloped to the ranch and back with help in that time. And if you'd tried to get an ambulance in here" — Darby gestured toward volcanic rocks sharp as broken glass — "or even a helicopter . . ."

"You think I feel guilty about Ben's death?" Cade slanted the rifle over one shoulder like a fishing pole. "I don't."

Oh, you do, too! Darby barely kept herself from yelling at him. Instead she wound the end of her ponytail around her index finger so tightly, it began cutting off her circulation.

Cade put his hat back on and pulled it low on his brow, before he said, "I just lost Megan's horse, yeah?"

"Yeah," she said, since there was no point arguing. She looked down at the black hair banding her finger and let it unwind.

No matter what Cade said, Darby knew he blamed himself, partly, for Ben Kato's death. And Megan's daily hostility wouldn't let Cade forget what had happened, either. But if things had happened the way Cade and Tutu had told her, why did Megan blame him?

"I'll take a look around for Tango before I ride back in."

"It's almost dark," she began, and when Cade shrugged, she added, "That's right, you can see in the dark."

"Like a cat," Cade admitted.

"Like an owl," Darby put in, thinking of her

family guardian, the *pueo*.

The correction must have pleased him, because Cade's tone was almost cheerful when he answered, "If you say so."

But then Darby remembered the pig she'd heard snuffling around last night.

"I think there are still pigs out here," Darby said.

"Of course there are," Cade said. "They're every-where. They're wrecking Hawaii."

"Could one have been at the stream? I saw tracks."

"Sure, and it's nothing to worry about," Cade said. "Things like what happened to Ben—they're really rare. Think of the size difference between a pig and a horse. Just steer clear of family groups, or pigs with rabies, and you'll be safe enough."

"Rabies?"

Cade nodded. "Almost any warm-blooded animal can get rabies. Even horses."

Chills claimed Darby's arms and she glanced toward Hoku.

"I guess I knew it wasn't just dogs," Darby said slowly. "But where would a pig get rabies?"

"From a mongoose, maybe," Cade suggested. "And some people say foxes escaped from 'Iolani a long time ago."

Darby thought of the clutter of gray cages near Hoku's home corral. Jonah had mentioned his father's ill-fated venture into the fox fur trade, but

Darby hadn't thought to ask what had become of the foxes.

"Rabies is, like, an inflammation of the brain, right?" Darby asked hesitantly.

"Yeah, it's spread by bites. Or, saliva, really. You can tell an animal's got it when it acts all nervous and excited. But that's not always easy.

"Once when I was with him, over by Mountain to the Sky, Jonah shot a mongoose he thought had it. Don't think I would have noticed. I always think of a mongoose as pretty excited, but he said it was unco-ordinated, chewing on nothing and drooling."

"Is that what horses do?" Darby asked, but part of her didn't really want to know.

"Yeah, but their back legs get paralyzed, too."

Darby winced. "And it's fatal?"

"Always, if they don't get medicine right away," Cade said. "But hey, the pig you saw wasn't—"

"I didn't exactly see it," Darby told him, and when Cade rolled his eyes, she snapped, "Not every-one can see in the dark, Cade. But I did see its tracks. And I heard it banging around."

"They're usually pretty quiet," Cade told her.

When his hand moved on his rifle stock, Darby tried to shut up. She didn't want Cade to kill any ani-mals because of her.

"Whatever it was, it didn't have rabies." Darby crossed her arms once she'd decided. "Think about it, Cade. Rabies is called hydrophobia, right?" she asked, but Cade just shrugged. "*Hydro* means 'water' and *phobia* means 'fear.' I know that much, and so anything with rabies would be afraid of water. And whatever I heard was sloshing around in the stream."

She was totally making this up, thinking aloud as she went along, and she didn't mind sounding bookish.

"It's pigs' nature to make wallows, and roll in the mud to keep off bugs or stay cool," Cade pointed out. "What animal's gonna let itself die of thirst with a stream right in front of it?"

"I'd give anything for a library right now," Darby said yearningly.

Cade's tone was gruff, but amused as he said, "With a lost horse and slobbering hog on the loose, you want a library?" Cade shook his head. "One thing you're good for, Darby Carter, is a laugh."

Darby deflected Cade's sarcasm with a smile. And when she thought of how she'd hoarded her chocolate, she didn't feel guilty at all.

Chapter 7

The next morning Darby and Hoku walked into the rain forest. At their intrusion, birds and insects had hushed. With no other noise to mask their movements, each step sounded as if they were crashing heedlessly through the vegetation.

Finally, they stopped on a wooded slope, picking an almost level spot where they had a view of the stream where the pink mare came to drink.

Darby sat with her notebook while Hoku rubbed her neck against a nearby tree. A pudgy, watermelon-colored bird glided near enough to study them, then landed on a branch. Down below, a gold-winged bird landed near the water and fluttered, taking a bath. Then other birds called and insects hummed, as if the forest had accepted them.

Unsettled by her conversation with Cade, Darby had stayed awake much of the night.

She'd been wrong about Cade. Ben had been riding Tango. Ben had ordered Cade to chase Tango, but after the first reflex obedience, he'd come back without Tango to help his mentor and Megan. It wasn't his fault that nothing could be done.

Tossing in the confinement of her sleeping bag, Darby had felt sick over her unwarranted suspicion.

If Megan wanted to be friends with Cade, she'd have to untangle their misunderstandings herself. Or go to Tutu.

Great-grandmothers, especially Darby's, had learned a thing or two about human nature, while Darby only knew about studying. And talking to horses. When she got them to talk back, then maybe she'd be a horse charmer.

I'm out of this, she'd declared, deciding to give up amateur detecting. Only then had she tumbled into a sound sleep.

Now Darby sat in the shade-strained sunlight, doing something she knew she could do. Homework. Hoku raised her head from inspecting a path-side plant and snorted, but her ears pointed away from the bird bathing below.

"Don't try to distract me," Darby said softly.

Jonah wanted her to list twenty-five things her horse did. As homework went, it was a piece of cake,

Darby thought. Working from memory, she started writing.

1. shivers skin
2. is picky about grass, so she carefully looks over what's there before taking bites
3. is not picky about hay, gulps whatever's close, even if she's walked on it
4. licks her lips, then sticks out her tongue

"I'm not sure why you do that," Darby whispered.

Hoku's head came up again, ears pricked, but not toward Darby. The filly concentrated on the patch of the rain forest surrounding the old man lichen rock. By the trail.

Darby looked, listened, and heard nothing that sounded out of place.

Of course Hoku would be watchful, she thought; every sound here was new.

Darby returned to her list.

5. sees things that aren't there
6. paws dirt
7. shakes head
8. scratches neck on fence
9. swings head around and uses teeth to scratch her back
10. uses hind hoof to reach up and scratch her chin

That last gesture made the filly look like a foal. She was so cute that Darby had to force herself to keep writing.

11. like a little kid, Hoku checks to see if I'm paying attention
12. goes to the bathroom in the same place every time
13. neighs at . . .

Nothing? That's the word Darby had been about to write when she heard someone coming through the forest. Some*one*, for sure, not some*thing*. She hadn't noticed signs of the wild pig since the night before last. She was sorry she'd mentioned it to Cade, because he'd probably told Jonah about it.

Darby waited in silence, but no one came out of the forest.

Shrugging, she looked at her list and saw that she'd made it halfway through her homework. There'd been no sign of Tango, and the shade that had cooled her had been replaced by tropical brightness that made her squint at the notebook paper.

Standing up to stretch, Darby awarded herself a break.

"Let's take you back to your corral, pretty girl."

Hoku yawned as if she'd been wakened, and followed as Darby led.

Quiet moments like this built as much trust as

brushing and blowing bubbles, Darby thought, and she wasn't going to throw away the progress she was making with her filly for the wild idea that had crept into her dreams last night.

She hadn't given up on the crazy project of mending Cade and Megan's friendship, only to take on a more insane and dangerous task.

She was *not* going to try to ride Hoku.

They'd reached the corral gate now. A trumpet-shaped flower on the vine winding around the fence bobbed against Darby's hand as she opened the gate. It might have been pecking her, saying, "liar, liar, liar."

As Darby looked down at the flower, something else caught her attention. Black hair was snagged on the splintery bottom board of the gate.

For a moment, her heart pounded. There was a low spot in the dirt and some animal had squeezed underneath.

It was probably a wirehaired black dog, Darby told herself. Not a wild pig. Those little black hairs could have been there for years.

Hoku's snort jerked Darby's attention back. The filly stared at her so intently, Darby glanced over her shoulders, but there was nothing there.

"You ready to go back inside?" Darby asked, and Hoku all but let herself into the corral.

But even when Darby had closed and locked the gate, Hoku watched her, signaling with her ears and eyes, as if she wanted to have an equine-human conversation.

I've been ridden before, Hoku's dark eyes told Darby.

"Yeah, too young," Darby said aloud. "It was a terrible experience. Like child abuse."

Hoku swished her tail, then tossed her chin toward her hindquarters, chasing away Darby's response. Or a bee.

I was ridden by a cruel man. Not by you. Not by someone I trust.

"Uh-huh, but that's the thing. Will you still trust me if I try to ride you too early?" Darby asked her horse.

Hoku stepped closer to the fence and Darby caught a teasing look in the filly's eyes. *If I let you climb on, then change my mind, who cares?*

"Good point," Darby told Hoku. "If I get bucked off, hurt, and no one's here to help me, I'd better die, 'cause if I don't, Jonah will kill me."

The filly trotted to the middle of the corral and stopped. As Hoku shook all over, her mane flipped from side to side, making an arc of light. Then she lowered herself to the ground and rolled.

Hoku felt so safe with Darby, she put herself in a vulnerable position—off all four hooves—in a strange place. Even as dust clouded her view of the forest, the horse was so relaxed, she groaned in pleasure, letting the ground massage her back.

Walk away from the corral, Darby ordered herself.

She did, glancing guiltily at the trees ringing the clearing.

She'd had way too many visitors to think she wouldn't be caught, if she kept talking to Hoku as if the filly were human. Or if she tried to ride her.

If I get bucked off, I'd better die, she'd just told Hoku.

Darby's cheeks heated in embarrassment, even though she was alone. How would that sound to anyone who knew of Ben Kato's fatal accident?

She'd better keep Ben's death in mind, Darby decided. If an expert horseman, a paniolo, could be killed in a riding accident, what could happen to her?

She'd think about that as she sat on the top fence rail of the corral.

Darby's boots had stopped walking. Hoku was a magnet, pulling her back to the corral. But she'd only watch her wild filly. And maybe finish her homework.

One thing was for sure: The filly's back was off-limits.

After a while, Darby could balance on the top rail of the fence, almost without thinking. It made her feel like a real cowgirl.

By noon, the sun stabbed through the canopy of leaves here, too, making Darby perspire. She squirmed as the tip of her ponytail tickled the damp nape of her neck. Balancing, she reached up and tightened it.

Hoku left her place across the corral and jogged straight to Darby so fast the sun struck rainbows on her golden coat.

"You're such a pretty girl," Darby said as Hoku brushed against her knees, then stopped a few steps past her.

What brought her over here? Darby wondered.

Her thoughts circled around an unlikely answer. To test the theory, Darby tightened her ponytail again.

Hoku backed up and turned her head to watch Darby.

Wow. Could Hoku be taking the movement as a signal to come close?

Darby was about to climb into the corral and try the gesture again, but Hoku trotted away. Darby tightened her ponytail. Here came Hoku again.

She wasn't imagining it. She might have blown a silent whistle only Hoku could hear.

This time the filly rubbed against Darby's leg more slowly, then trotted off, giving a little buck as if she liked this game.

For a fourth time, Darby tightened a ponytail already stinging her scalp from pulling her hair, and Hoku jumped her way, nuzzled Darby's leg, and slid her head under it.

Darby swallowed hard, as if that would stop her heart's pounding. Her ankle rested on the other side of Hoku's neck.

She didn't move. She barely breathed as she remembered her first sight of Hoku running on the snowy Nevada range. Then she recalled Hoku on the night she'd pranced and bucked before galloping into the Hawaiian darkness.

Hoku loved to run. Her wild heart told her she'd been born to do it. Yet Jonah insisted Hoku stay in small corrals. Hoku couldn't possibly know a rider was her passport out of confinement, could she?

But if I rode you, we could go running together, Darby thought. *We could gallop as far and fast as you like, because if you're carrying me, I can remind you to go back home.*

Darby looked at the gate. What if she started by riding inside the corral?

She'd just tighten her ponytail, slip onto Hoku's back, and ride in circles until she was certain they understood each other. What would be the harm in that?

Darby's fear dropped away as she and Hoku stared at each other. Trust went both ways. If Hoku trusted Darby to sit on her back, she would have to trust Hoku not to throw her.

Hoku lifted her head. A longing neigh drifted from her lips.

Yes! Darby thought. *Do it!*

Chapter 8

As she watched her horse, Darby's senses were turned up higher than they'd ever been before.

That was probably why she heard footsteps, even though the person approaching was working at stealth.

Close, quick, and light, the feet came on.

Darby jumped off the top rail and onto the ground outside the corral.

"Megan!" Darby clapped her hands together.

She'd missed her chance to ride Hoku, but there'd be another. She was sure of it.

She was excited by the sight of her friend. Until she got a good look at her.

Megan looked tired, which was strange. Megan

was usually pep personified, and a total athlete. Usually, Darby thought her friend's thick russet hair and agile-cat strides would make her a TV star if she did commercials for protein bars or an expensive gym. But not today.

Now Megan walked a little off-balance, carrying something by its handle, and her face was flushed.

Megan hadn't returned her greeting or taken off her dark glasses. And her hair . . . Megan never had a bad hair day. Or if she did, she hid it under a boyish cap that somehow made her look even more feminine.

"What's wrong?" Darby asked. "Did something happen?"

Megan ignored Darby's questions. She swung the drink jug she carried.

"I brought some lemonade. I wish we hadn't eaten all of m-my paniolo pizza." Megan's voice caught as if she'd been crying, but she plowed ahead as if it hadn't. "What did you think of it?"

"I loved it, but you can't—I mean, you didn't come out here to ask me that."

Tutu had told Darby that Megan hadn't come to the rain forest camp since the accident, but suddenly here she was.

Silently, Darby vowed not to start meddling again, but she had to wonder.

"No," Megan said, "I didn't." She set the jug on the ground, took off her dark glasses to show eyes swollen from crying, and crossed her arms.

"I had a fight with Cade, and then my mom g-got into it." Megan stopped and cleared her throat. "It was bad, but at least my mom said I could skip school today."

"She did?" Darby asked, aghast. Even in the short time she'd been at 'Iolani Ranch, she'd learned Auntie Cathy put school before almost everything.

"Yeah, it was a miracle. She said the fresh air would do me good."

Darby tried to sound casual when she asked, "So what happened?"

"I was getting ready for school when Cade yelled from outside. He was standing at the bottom of our stairs, with all the dogs bouncing around him. He looked so excited.

"And he's yelling, 'We're going to catch your horse!' Just like that. It's been almost two years. He said he'd found Tango in the forest not far from where—" Megan broke off, shaking her head. "No, he really said *you'd* found Tango."

It was just a reflex, Darby thought as Megan flashed her an accusatory look. Megan blamed Darby for uncovering the tender part of her that still mourned her father, but the look was quickly replaced by a wry smile.

"After all this time, you just go out there and Tango comes to you. I guess you really are—"

"Don't say it," Darby interrupted. "Tango was looking for *you*."

A look of hope crossed Megan's face before she asked, "What makes you think so?"

"The bubbles. She didn't come into the clearing and stay until I started blowing bubbles for Hoku."

"Good," Megan said. She stared into the forest until she looked almost peaceful. Then she shook her head and said, "But I've still messed things up at home. Big time. When Cade said he'd have Biscuit saddled when I got home from school and we could get Kit to help us track down Tango, he looked all hopeful, like when he was a kid. That poor little kid. . . ."

In that minute, it was so quiet, Darby heard the claws of a lizard climbing the tree next to her. But she barely glanced at it.

"I asked him," Megan said with self-loathing, "if he hadn't already done enough."

Darby couldn't help wincing and Megan nodded. She knew how cruel that had been.

"And that's when my mother got into it," Megan went on. "So then I yelled at her, saying she hadn't been there, so what did she know, and I must have been pretty loud, because that's what sent the dogs slinking away and then Kimo drove up, got out of his truck, took in the whole stupid situation, and said, 'What's shakin', Mekana? You skip school, you gonna end up like me.'"

After the perfect imitation of Kimo, Megan let out a gigantic sigh and fell silent.

Finally, Darby tried to distract her friend. She looked at the jug Megan had set down between them.

"So, this is lemonade," Darby said.

Megan made a gulping noise that was half sob and half laugh.

"Yeah, Mom made me bring it, so that I"—her voice caught, but she kept going—"stay hydrated." She used both hands to wipe her cheeks. "Really, I didn't know I had this many tears left in me."

Megan's lower lip trembled, but Darby would bet Megan wasn't just feeling sorry for herself, but for Cade, too. And she must be missing her father all over again.

But Darby didn't say that. She'd given up meddling. Still, she felt like she should do something.

Casting around for a way to make Megan feel better, Darby suddenly knew what to say.

"I have chocolate."

"It's too sweet to have with the lemonade, and I can't play soccer today, so I won't be able to work it off, and besides . . ." Megan rolled her eyes. "Darby."

"What?"

"I know my eyes are all swollen up like . . . a stomped-on toad, so you don't have to try so hard not to look at them."

"A stomped-on toad?" Darby repeated.

"You're from that other West," Megan said, gesturing vaguely toward the mainland. "I thought all you guys talked that way."

"Not me," Darby said. "Besides, no one's out here but us, and your eyes aren't that noticeable —"

"You are such a bad liar," Megan said flatly. "And just for that, I *am* going to eat your chocolate."

Megan stalked toward the hut, and Darby shouted, "Not all of it!"

"Try to stop me!" Megan growled in mock menace.

She lifted Darby's backpack and gave it a shake.

"First you have to find it!" Darby dared, but, as it turned out, she ended up helping Megan do just that. And they ate all the chocolate together.

Chapter 9

Late-afternoon rain showered the rain forest. Full of chocolate and lemonade, the girls retreated to Darby's house of ferns, sat on her spread-out sleeping bag, and watched the raindrops turn a spiderweb just outside into a jeweled net.

"I saw a happy-face spider," Darby said.

"They're kind of cool, huh?"

Megan sounded sleepy, so Darby just nodded, then sat silently as raindrops drummed the leaves and branches.

Darby loved the warm tropical rainstorms that bathed the island.

Back on the ranch, the cowboys would work right through the showers, because they happened at least once a day. Darby wondered if they were wearing slickers now, or just moving under cover to drink coffee while they repaired and polished tack.

Thunder grumbled beyond the treetops and Darby soaked up the moody atmosphere of waiting out the rain while she listened to Hoku splashing in the puddle forming in her corral.

"I haven't been back here for a long time," Megan spoke up. "Not since my dad died."

"I'm sorry," Darby said, wishing she could think of something better to say.

"Mom always says he died doing what he loved." Megan sighed, "But, you know? That doesn't make me feel much better."

Wind squalled through the clearing, spraying water on the girls' faces, and they both scooted farther back into the shelter.

"I don't see me walking home in this," Megan said sourly.

"You walked?"

"Most of the way. We're not supposed to bring horses in here without a reason."

Darby nodded, remembering Cade had said the same thing.

"So, if you don't mind me hanging around for a while . . ."

"Mind? I think it would be cool if you could spend the night!" Darby said.

"I don't know about that. . . ." Megan glanced

around the shelter, raising her eyebrow as if these were awfully tight quarters for two.

"It'll be dark soon, and you shouldn't go out there. There've been wild pigs around, I think, and Cade said they could have rabies," Darby said, even though she knew she was exaggerating Cade's words.

"Cade . . ." For the first time Megan sounded understanding. "He's paranoid about wild pigs. Of course, so am I."

Darby remembered when they'd ridden into Crimson Vale together and Megan thought she'd spotted a black boar. She'd turned pale and shaky, and nearly lost control of Conch, the grulla horse she was riding.

"Do you know," Megan said, as if she couldn't believe her own words, "I used to be really afraid of Cade?"

Darby's breath hitched in her throat. She coughed, wishing she'd stop, because she wanted to hear more.

"Afraid?" Darby repeated breathlessly.

"In that hysterical, slumber-party kind of way." Megan tried to make light of her confession. "I'm older than him, so it didn't make any sense."

"Not that much older," Darby said, making an excuse for her friend. "But what scared you about him?"

"My parents—" Megan stopped and sighed. "To be fair, I totally misunderstood what they were trying to tell me. My mom said, because Cade came from an abusive home, we had to help him learn there were other ways to solve problems besides violence."

"That makes sense," Darby said.

"Yeah, but she said violence had been 'pounded into him.' That scared me, made me stupid and paranoid.

"And then my dad said—" Megan broke off again, wearing a bittersweet smile. "He was a real paniolo, you know, like Jonah. And Cade, too, I guess. Did you know Cade's the one who told my dad and Jonah about Tango? He'd seen her running up in Crimson Vale with Black Lava and thought she'd make a perfect horse for me.

"I tried to be grateful, but I was still scared of him. So I avoided Cade and said snotty things, and finally my dad took me aside and told me Cade was like a tree with aerial roots, just splaying out in the air, looking for a place to sink down into the earth. And he said Manny, Cade's stepfather, kept coming along and hacking off those roots with a knife, every time they started to find a safe place. Something like that. And he said I could help Cade's roots reach the ground or keep hacking them off. It was my choice."

Darby sighed. "Wow, I wish I'd met your dad."

"Well, you might have understood him," Megan said. "I was just too shallow."

"No," Darby said.

"All I knew was, Cade was this weird kid with a

lump on his jaw, who was always carrying around a knife or a gun—" Megan broke off and tried to make a joke. "Is it any wonder he didn't go to Lehua High? They would have arrested him!" Megan shook her head then, probably at how dense she'd been, Darby thought. "I just didn't get it."

"What kid would?" Darby asked. "I can sit here and think, oh, he was protecting himself, not threatening you, but if he'd come into my house? I would've been scared to death."

Megan shrugged.

"Wait, you know what?" Darby had just remembered something. "When I first got here and I saw Cade, a guy slightly older than me, with this gun on his saddle, it totally creeped me out."

Gray dusk pressed in between the trees. Half laying on the sleeping bag, propped up on her elbow, Megan stared into the twilight, then looked straight at Darby. "You know what happened, don't you?"

Because Tutu's account had been so brief, and Cade's so sad, and because, to be totally honest, she wanted to see how the three stories fit together, Darby said, "I know some of it."

"It was supposed to be this wonderful day," Megan said. "My dad and Cade were working Tango around cattle to see how she'd do, and if she did all right, I was going to try her that afternoon with some of Jonah's calves. He said Tango was 'cowy' and would make a good cutting horse.

"That night, we were all going into town, to have dinner out, and—what was that?"

Darby had heard the sound, too.

"Sort of like little tiny bells?" she whispered.

The rain had stopped while they were talking, but it still dripped off thousands of branches.

Then she heard a creak.

"Hoku?" Darby called. Her filly might have made that sound by leaning against the fence. She could have, except that Darby heard Hoku's hooves trotting restlessly around her corral.

Something hard struck wood. Startled once more, Megan's shoulder collided with Darby's. The girls flinched apart, but only by a few inches.

The far-off musical sound came again.

"Something's out there," Darby said.

"Whatever it is just tripped," Megan said sarcastically.

"No, it's probably just birds." Darby clasped her hands together to keep them from shaking.

"In the night?"

"There are lots of birds out here," Darby insisted.

"In the *dark*?" Megan replied, even more insistent.

"Haven't you noticed all the birds?" Darby wished Megan would just agree with her.

"None that trip over downed branches."

"Night's not quite here," Darby protested, but then a muddy squelch came to them both and the girls faced each other. "Okay, it's not a bird."

"It's also not trying to be quiet," Megan observed.

Hoku gave an uneasy whinny.

"Your horse hears it, too," Megan said. For the first time, she sounded worried.

"It could be Cade," Darby said. "He's come out to bring me messages from Jonah. And you know how he's supposed to have really good night vision."

But after that, it was quiet for so long, they both relaxed.

When Megan spoke again, she sounded younger. "He could have saved my dad, you know, by handling the cattle better, or riding between the boar and Tango—"

"Megan, he was just a kid." Darby didn't mean to defend Cade, but Megan wasn't being fair. "What do you expect of a thirteen-year-old?"

"You were twelve when you saved Hoku."

"It's not the same thing. No vicious animal was after us. Nothing was chasing Hoku except a helicopter, and it had already flown away, over the mountains. I didn't do anything but wait with her until help came."

"He could have done that, instead of riding after Tango." Megan sounded both heartbroken and bitter. "My dad was his friend, his mentor. Cade could have done what you did for that horse—just stayed with him."

Darby tried to calm her friend by saying, "You don't know that."

"Yeah, she does."

Darby gasped at the sudden male voice.

"She was there." Cade walked into camp. His dark green poncho flowed around him. His spurs made a faint chiming.

Darby took a deep breath to steady herself, but if Megan felt startled, she didn't show it.

"I was just leaving," Megan said, but Cade shot her a look that said he'd have to be pretty stupid to believe that, since the girls were clearly settled down for the night.

Darby was glad Megan stayed put, but for a minute she felt invisible.

Megan's and Cade's eyes were locked in a silent war, until Cade said, "He told me to ride after Tango."

Megan didn't answer, didn't move.

"You heard him," Cade reminded her.

"He didn't know what he was saying!" Megan snapped.

"He knew," Cade told her. "Tango was your—"

"Besides that, you didn't get Tango!"

Cade drew in a deep breath, then let it out. "I would have. I was following the blood drops on the leaves and dirt—" He paused as Megan's arms jerked up and clamped around herself. "But I heard you—"

"Oh yeah, this is my fault," Megan said. "Go ahead and say it. If I hadn't screamed when I saw the pig go between Tango's front legs, Dad wouldn't have looked at me and lost his concentration. And if I hadn't been crying over my dad, asking him not to die, you would have kept riding after Tango."

"Megan," Cade said, his voice filled with sympathy.

Megan made him stop, not by yelling this time, but she held out a hand, a sign for Cade to halt.

"You didn't even cry," Megan accused him, and Darby, looking between the two, thought this must be a new weapon in Megan's arsenal, because Cade's eyes seemed to darken in pain before he turned away.

But he didn't leave.

Darby wanted to say something to keep her friends talking. But what? Jonah had been speaking of horses when he ordered her to trust her mana.

She pictured Tango standing right where Cade was now. Darby had been in the lean-to, and for the first time she'd seen the extent of scars so deep, the mare's pink hair hadn't covered them.

"Neither of you could have kept Tango from going over backward," Darby said quietly.

Cade wheeled to stare at her. Megan's voice rose in an outrage, as she yelped, "What," and both of them glared at her.

"When that boar went between Tango's front legs, he slashed her with his tusks," Darby said.

"Darby, I know you're trying to be nice, but just—"

"No, go ahead," Cade told her.

"Yesterday I was close enough to Tango to see her

underbelly, and she still has scars. Long ones.

"I'm not a super rider. I know that. But Tango had to be in pain, and terrified. I keep thinking about it, sort of from her point of view, and no matter what your dad did, I don't think he could have stopped Tango from going over backward.

"The boar was ripping through her skin. If she tried to run right or left, he would've stayed with her. Bolting forward would have rammed his tusks in deeper. How else was she supposed to get away from him?"

Megan flashed a questioning look at Cade.

"It coulda been that way," he said. "I remember thinking there was a lot of blood, when I was following her."

"But we would have seen it happen," Megan said. "Wouldn't we?"

"The scars are on her belly," Darby said, miming where they'd be on her own body.

"And we were both watching Ben, not Tango," Cade said.

"So, there really wasn't . . ."

Anything that anyone could do, Darby silently finished the thought. She was pretty sure that was the rest of Megan's sentence, but Megan wasn't ready to let go of what she thought she remembered yet.

Still, Darby felt that some of the tension in the clearing had lifted. She almost held her breath until Cade asked, "Megan, do you want a ride home? You know Joker will carry double."

"I left Biscuit at Tutu's," Megan said, and it didn't sound like an excuse.

"How about a ride as far as Tutu's cottage, then?"

Now Cade's generosity sounded forced, and Darby wished she could make him stop while things were relatively tranquil.

"If this downpour gets going, it'll be a nasty ride back to Sun House," he added.

"I'm staying with Darby tonight, Cade. My mom knows."

"Okay, then," Cade said, nodding. And then he turned, but not the way he'd wheeled around before. As he walked away, the chiming of his spurs lingered.

The shelter was crowded, but Megan dozed off before Darby had even turned the lantern down.

Darby lay awake for only a few minutes. She felt satisfied. Megan and Cade were on their way to being friends again. But her mind kept returning to Megan's shrill accusation.

You didn't even cry! Megan had said. Cade had looked ashamed, but maybe if you were a boy whose stepfather broke your jaw and your mother didn't rescue you, your only chance to win against a monster like Manny was to refuse to give him the satisfaction of seeing you cry.

Wasn't it possible Cade had learned to control his

feelings? And Megan had been too shocked and distraught to see what he'd felt for her father—his friend and mentor?

Drifting off to sleep, Darby heard thunder moving away. It reminded her of Jonah, talking of his mana's silent thunder, and then it reminded her of hoofbeats.

She sighed and smiled, and once more, in her dreams, she rode Hoku.

Chapter 10

"My eyes hurt."

The three words brought Darby awake, even though it was so early. Silvery mist hid everything outside her shelter.

"Can you see?" Darby croaked, then cleared her throat.

"It's just from crying," Megan said, giving Darby's shoulder a shove. "I'm not used to it. My head hurts, too. I'm going to go home and apologize to my mom and hope she fusses over me and gives me aspirin before she forces me to go to school."

"You could just be suffering from a chocolate overdose."

Megan moaned. "Don't tell me that's all we had for dinner last night."

"Okay," Darby agreed.

They both laughed until Megan sucked in a breath. "Thanks for mentioning that stuff last night. About Tango's scars."

"No big deal," Darby said.

A knee slammed against Darby's back as Megan maneuvered her long legs from her niche in the shelter.

"I'll move," Darby said.

"Don't."

"Ow!" Darby said, using her elbows to pull herself out of the way.

"Sorry," Megan said. "It's too early. Go back to sleep."

"I'm not going to let you go alone," Darby protested.

"It's not like I don't know my way to Tutu's cottage," Megan said. "But you— Well, not to be mean, but in this mist, you'd have a hard time finding your way back. I'd rather not worry about you."

Darby had a vision of herself wandering in circles, bumping into trees, and conceded that Megan was right.

"Okay, but take something to eat," Darby said, pushing an apple and some jerky into Megan's hands before she was ready to leave.

"About Cade—I don't know what to say about

how mean I was." Megan swallowed so hard, Darby heard her. "Have you ever lost someone you love?"

Darby felt almost guilty for shaking her head "no."

"You're lucky," Megan said. "Just hope it doesn't happen until you're old enough to handle it. I'm not."

"You're not doing such a bad job," Darby said.

"Yeah, I only traumatized a kid who was already in bad shape."

"I think Cade's tougher than that."

"I hope so," Megan said, tucking her shirt into her jeans. Then she looked up. "Hey, you know, I heard Kit and Kimo talking about you. You know what Kimo said?"

"I'm afraid to hear it," Darby said, because as much as she liked Kimo, her strongest memory was him telling her *mo bettah you ask* when she'd messed up instead of asking for help with the horses.

"No, it's good. They were talking about you coming out here on your own and Kimo said, 'That Darby, she's one smart, can-do *keiki*.'" Megan broke off to touch her lips, gently. "I could do Kimo's voice better if it weren't so early. Anyway, Kit nodded about ten times and then, you know, in that slow buckaroo way he does? He said, 'Yup, the can-do kid. That 'bout sums it up.'"

Darby managed a self-conscious mutter. "They didn't say that."

"Like I'd make it up," Megan said, snagging the

handle of the empty lemonade jug.

Megan had taken a few steps, and Darby had set-tled back down in her sleeping bag when Megan said, "Darby, are you sure?"

Darby raised up on one elbow. "Sure?"

"That the horse is Tango, I mean. Does she have a little whirly thing"—Megan touched her fore-head—"here?"

"Yeah, she did," Darby said, smiling. "And you'd better come back soon, because even though you'd probably have a lot easier time catching her than I would, I'll probably try it alone."

"You will?"

"I can't help it." Darby shrugged. "I just know I will."

Invisible in the fog, a bird made a clacking noise from a branch overhead.

"I'll be back tomorrow," Megan said finally, and as she hiked off into the foggy forest, Darby raised her fist in victory.

After Megan had gone, Darby found that her intense desire to ride Hoku had faded. Cade and Megan had already provided way too much excitement. Emotional stuff always tired Darby out more than physical exertion, and what she really wanted was to sit and read.

She'd brought along a book from Jonah's library. It was about Hawaiian wildlife, and she'd taken it into Hoku's corral to read while she kept the filly company.

It wasn't easy to find a dry spot where she could sit and read comfortably. Yesterday's rain had turned the low spots into puddles or bogs.

Hoku had found the dip under her corral gate and decided it was pretty amusing to dig and splash and turn her fiery coat mud brown. The filly had made the big puddle so deep, Darby knew she should fill it with dirt before they left at the end of the week.

At last, Darby found the perfect patch of sunlight—not too hot, just cozy—on the highest point inside Hoku's corral, directly across from the gate where she'd been sitting yesterday.

She haltered Hoku and snapped on her lead rope, threw out some hay for the horse to munch, then settled with the book and read.

Suddenly, they both heard snuffling.

Darby jammed the postcard she was using as a bookmark into the book. She set the book aside, dropped the lead rope, climbed the fence, and clinging to the top rail, scanned the clearing, trying to see where the sound was coming from.

She was just in time to see a black pig lurch up from the stream bed, drooling.

His four tusks were the bone yellow of a smoker's teeth. Two tusks on top and two on the bottom, all curved out, then pointing up, except one, which looked like it had broken off in a fight.

Jonah had been right. This was no fairy-tale pig.

Bristles on his shoulders looked bushy as a lion's mane. His backbone's crest of coarse hair had blondish points. His hairless tail wasn't curly, and the way his pointed ears stuck straight up would have made him look alert, except that he was weaving and stumbling as he came toward the corral.

He must be sick, Darby thought, because wildlife came out at dawn or dusk, and this wasn't either one. He wasn't swift and agile like a wild creature should be, either. He staggered.

The pig made a sound that was more bawl than oink, and Darby felt glad that she and Hoku were safe inside the corral.

She glanced at her horse. Frozen with curiosity on the far side of the pen, the filly stared, then she made a strange circular swing of her head and bared her teeth.

Just stay where you are, Darby thought. It was her job, not Hoku's, to scare off the pig.

"Get out of here!" Darby yelled, but the boar only increased his pace until he was running.

He slammed into the fence. Darby almost lost her grip as the impact telegraphed through the fence rails.

"Shoo! Go away!" She bellowed loudly enough that the animal should be terrified, but he only threw his head to one side, masking himself in his own slobber.

Darby dropped back inside the corral and

scooped up some small rocks. The first one she threw hit the fence. Another arced over the top rail, but the pig ignored it. Then, grunting and shoving his face along the ground in just the way she'd imagined pigs would root, his nose splattered into Hoku's favorite puddle.

When Darby saw the black snout reach under the fence, she used both hands to throw the rest of the rocks. They rained down on the fence and dirt, but one must have hit the pig's eye, because he blinked rapidly and was still.

For a few seconds, Darby thought she'd driven him off, but she was wrong.

The boar angled his entire head under the fence, then squealed at the tight squeeze he'd gotten himself into.

The ear-piercing sound made her feel sorry for the animal.

What now? Would he remain pinned there, or would the mud give way enough that he could jam the rest of his body through? Would he come after her and Hoku?

Be sensible, Darby told herself. The pig was huge. He wouldn't make it through the space between the fence rail and the ground. Even if the fence broke and he made it in, she could climb out.

Wrong, she thought. She would not leave Hoku. What did a range-reared mustang know about a rain-forest pig?

Even though the boar would have to be crazy to charge an animal so much bigger, he was sick. She didn't have to be a vet to see that. And if he was sick with rabies, his brain was inflamed. He wouldn't know he was doing something dangerous.

The whole fence rocked as the boar shoved against it.

Hoku lowered her head. Her ears flicked in all directions. She was angry at this intruder, but she didn't know what to do about him.

"It's okay, girl," Darby lied to her horse. Then she tried to make a plan.

If the boar got through, he'd run away from the gate. Then she'd dash over, grab Hoku's lead, and — would she have time to unbolt the gate and slip through before the boar swung his bulk around and barreled after them?

It would take about a minute, but the boar was having a hard time handling his own body. She and Hoku might make it. Might.

Hoku reared, striking at the fence. Then she circled toward Darby, rolling her eyes before she made a feint at jumping.

The filly had the right idea. If the pig came in here, she'd jump out. But the corral had been built with such escape in mind. The fence was tall. If Hoku got hung up on the top rail . . .

Darby shuddered. Then she climbed the fence.

"You stay there," she ordered the filly.

Darby began crab-walking on the second highest rail. She stopped when she got close enough to have a really good view of the pig. He'd redirected his shoving to the first section of fence to the right of the gate.

That meant . . . Darby ignored the squealing and huffing just below her and tried to focus. If she opened the bolt on the gate, but didn't swing it wide, she'd save time. She and Hoku could be a few more seconds ahead of those tusks.

She slid open the bolt, and for a second, Darby was sure the boar hadn't even noticed. But he had. His narrow head lay against the ground and one eye tracked her movement. The fence swayed from his efforts, but Darby stayed balanced until one of his tusks snagged on the wood.

If she hadn't seen it happen, she wouldn't have grabbed on to the fence with all her might. As it was, she swayed on the gate as it swung open and slammed closed.

But the pig didn't realize he had a way in.

Darby made her way back to Hoku, gave the filly a quick smooch as she passed her, then stopped at the rail-top spot where Hoku had come to her, begging to be ridden, yesterday.

For an instant, she considered trying it, but then she gave up. This wasn't the right time to try to ride Hoku. Another horse, rider, and boar could end up tangled on the rain-forest floor.

Darby climbed down off the fence and tightened her ponytail.

The rain forest was silent, as if the birds were watching the boar's noisy performance and her quiet one.

Hoku gave a worried nicker, then came to her.

Grabbing Hoku's lead rope, Darby glanced toward the pig. He'd rocked one of his shoulders underneath the fence. She wasn't sure, but she thought that was the widest part of his body.

Darby filled her left hand with rocks, and wrapped the tangerine-and-white lead rope around her right.

She clucked at Hoku, but the filly's neck and flanks were dark with sweat.

"It's me, girl," Darby cooed to the filly. "Don't look at him. Just me."

She hated standing here, waiting for the boar to make the first move, but there was no other choice.

As soon as she saw where he was going, she'd distract him by throwing rocks and pray she could cling to Hoku's lead rope long enough to get her through the gate. After that, if the filly ran, she'd have to let go.

They both looked around at the pig's pained squeal. With a gigantic effort, he'd thrust his second shoulder under the fence.

Darby heard his back hooves paddling in the mud, but her eyes focused on her filly's sweating back.

She leaned away from the fence and threaded her fingers through Hoku's golden mane.

"Girl?" she said, but the filly didn't seem to hear.

Hoku's eyes rolled white and blind with fear as she looked back over her shoulder.

The pig was inside the corral.

Chapter 11

Between one heartbeat and the next Darby realized the boar had struggled to his feet. He was headed straight for them.

"This way," she told Hoku, then gently moved the lead rope.

The mustang spun away and hit the end of the rope with such force, Darby lost her balance. She only kept herself from falling by grabbing a handful of Hoku's mane.

Disoriented by all the commotion, the black boar swayed, lifting his snout into the air. He trotted toward them and Hoku stared with stricken fascination.

The rocks. Darby tried throwing one past the

boar to see what he would do.

Nothing. No, wait, his reaction was delayed, but he grunted and turned toward the spot where the rock had landed.

As plans went, Darby thought, hers wasn't much. She'd try to lure him closer with the rocks, and then, when she couldn't hold Hoku anymore—and that moment was coming soon—they'd dart for the gate. Once it was locked behind them with the boar inside, maybe she could lead Hoku to Tutu's cottage, and then home to 'Iolani Ranch, to get Jonah to come confront the pig.

Part of her plan worked. The pig lunged toward them and fell onto his bristly right shoulder. Darby had time to throw only one rock and see that the pig stared at the noise it made, before Hoku bolted.

Nearly running already, the filly veered around the pig, and all at once Darby knew she had to move faster. If she didn't, Hoku would jump over the gate, and Darby would be slammed into it.

She heard the pig breathing loudly behind her, but Darby didn't look back to see which direction it was headed.

It didn't matter. She had to get the gate open. It was unlatched, it should only take a second, but Hoku reared in frustration.

Darby clung to the rope with both hands, afraid to let go. But she had to. They were too close to the fence. Hoku thought she could jump, but it would be more like climbing. She'd be hurt in the attempt.

Darby opened her hands. She let the rope drop, and jerked the gate open. She didn't let her attention wander long enough to see where the pig was, just held the gate wide enough for Hoku to shoulder through.

She wanted to grab the rope close to Hoku's halter, but the filly was moving so fast, Darby was lucky to catch the last few inches of the rope as it trailed behind her horse.

Momentum and Darby's unplanned-for weight caused the filly to scrabble with all four hooves to keep from crashing into Darby's shelter.

Tall ferns whipped Darby's legs as Hoku spun to the right.

"Whoa," Darby yelled, but her feet were barely touching the ground. She couldn't get into a stance where she could brace and stop the filly.

"Whoa!" Darby yelled again, but Hoku only moved faster.

She had to let go or be dragged to death. Hoku jumped a rock, dodged a tree, and Darby somehow stayed with her.

Vines lashed Darby's face. A cacophony of red birds exploded like a fountain before them. Hoku zigzagged around an old tree trunk and then slowed for a few steps.

"Okay," Darby gasped. Forcing her eyes to see past wind-whipped tears, Darby realized they were at the edge of the *kipuka*. Sharp lava rock lay just ahead.

A blast of salt wind struck them and Hoku gave a shrill neigh. But she didn't bolt. Hooves tapping, she crossed the lava carefully, dragging in deep draughts of salt air as if it were water.

"We can do it, baby. Just be careful. Good girl."

Darby wanted to stop, *had* to stop if she planned to breathe anytime soon, but this was not the place to insist.

Once they reached the rock-studded dirt on the other side, she'd make a grab for Hoku's halter and focus all her strength and mana and anything else she could think of on the task of leading her into that grove of trees, just ahead.

She tried. Darby's shoulders, elbows, and wrists ached from pulling, but the filly wouldn't stop. Darby forgot all about being a horse charmer. She just tried to be heavy.

The trees were wider apart in this grove, but it was dark. And growing darker, even though it was the middle of the day. Where was Hoku taking her? She couldn't let the filly get a second wind or she'd lose her in a place she didn't even recognize.

Suddenly, they burst out of the trees into the sunlight. Green hills unrolled before them.

Darby groaned as Hoku released a piercing neigh. The sorrel filly had longed for open country like the sagebrush roamed by her sire and all the other wild horses that had come before her.

Eden, Darby thought, or something close to it. But surely this was where she'd lose her horse. Hoku would shake off the human weight at the end of her lead rope and glide into an endless gallop.

Darby didn't realize she was dragging in painful breaths, one after the other, trying to catch up, until a second set of hooves pounded up behind them, and she gasped.

Tango! With joyous snorts, the two horses bumped shoulders. Darby gasped and gripped Hoku's rope still tighter with the raw palms of her hands. They were at the edge of a steep sidehill and she didn't want Hoku to plunge down it, leading Tango in a game of chase.

But the two horses stopped, striking out in a mock fight. Darby ducked away from Tango's black hooves, and that was when it happened.

The horses veered apart, then came back together. Darby finally tripped, fell, lost her grip on the rope, and rolled.

When she came to a stop, she was able to raise her head enough to see Hoku and Tango leap a narrow gully. A spray of brown birds rose before them and they loped with sideways steps, trying to watch a wild turkey.

They were beautiful, and they were so gone.

Darby made herself stand up. Dizzy from her run with Hoku, she struggled for balance.

Where was she? The salt wind meant she was

closer to the ocean, right? They could be near Crimson Vale—and the wild stallion Black Lava.

What if he'd wandered inland in search of mares again and took Hoku?

Far off, the two horses crested a shoulder of emerald-green grass. The last she saw of Hoku and Tango, the horses were running as a pair.

She might have watched a little longer, but just then her knees buckled from the hammering they'd taken. Darby lost her balance and slipped on the slick grass of the sidehill.

Trying to stop, she grabbed at vines, flowers, and dirt, everything that passed beneath her. Then she let go and let herself roll.

Once, her elbows and knees collided with a clutter of lichen-covered rocks at the edge of a cliff. The collision slowed her, but she didn't stop.

She tumbled on, until she hit bottom with a splat.

Darby lay facedown in mud, thought quickly enough to turn her head and not breathe it in, then closed her eyes and assessed her body.

Her head hurt. When she opened her eyes, she felt so dizzy she feared she might throw up, so she closed them.

Why was her pulse pounding in her ears instead of her wrists? She didn't know, but she was encouraged that flexing her fingers didn't make her yelp in pain. Neither did stirring her legs or shrugging her shoulders.

So far, so good, but the fact remained that she was lying in mud. It oozed against her shins, knees, thighs, and it might be welling up the legs of her shorts.

Darby swallowed hard and tried opening her eyes again.

She lay at the bottom of a hill, looking up.

She wanted to stand, but orbs of blue, orange, and violet lights danced before her eyes, keeping her light-headed.

Darby raised her chin out of the mud and looked ahead. Even with her eyelashes barely raised, she could tell she was sighting up another hill.

Which one had she rolled down? Why hadn't she just gone limp and given in to rolling instead of trying to stop herself at that cluster of—

Hoku! There, just past the green rocks she'd pushed away from, back up the hill, stood Hoku!

The filly blinked down at her, tail swishing with curiosity. When Hoku tossed her head, her sun-shot mane looked like a halo.

"You didn't leave me."

Chapter 12

*H*er lips felt stiff, so they were probably caked with mud, but it didn't matter. People would pay plenty for a bath of healthy Hawaiian minerals, she thought, smiling weakly.

And it didn't matter that her clothes were soaked and dirty. She had others.

What mattered was that Hoku hadn't left her.

The wild filly had trusted Darby to get them out of the corral, away from the boar. And she hadn't taken the chance to escape!

As happy as she was, Darby couldn't push away another sickening surge of dizziness. She closed her eyes and gloried in the fact that she hadn't schooled the instincts out of Hoku. Jonah would be proud, if she ever got up the nerve to tell him.

Darby didn't know how long she lay there, hiding behind the darkness of her eyelids, listening while Hoku grazed.

When she was finally feeling better, Darby gathered her strength to open her eyes again. Before she did, something brushed her fingertips.

It felt warm, but it was as coarse as the bristles on her hairbrush. She heard a small gumping sound and something round as a puppy's belly bumped her face, then moved away.

Darby opened her eyes to see the slick, black nose of a piglet. It studied her with tiny, eager eyes, and Darby felt a smile begin on her mud-smeared face.

Then she stopped. It was cute, all right, but a piglet like this one had caused Ben Kato's death.

Crazy, rabid pigs might not travel in family groups, but she'd bet this little piggy had a mother, and maybe even a father, nearby.

Sun baked Darby's back and Hoku's teeth made a vigorous snatching sound.

Don't panic. Darby scoffed at her cowardice. She had to be exaggerating the danger she was in. She simply wasn't the kind of person who faced mortal peril twice in one day.

Trying to dredge up some of the hidden courage Jonah thought she possessed, Darby raised her head and looked around until her neck trembled. She made her eyes sweep so far to the right they burned.

Then, she did the same thing in the other direction.

Tutu had said this was a good place to practice using other senses besides sight, so she let her head down and tried her best.

The piglet snuffled. Mud splattered her hand, so he must be rolling. Wallowing, Cade had called it. The grass smelled freshly mown, like a Saturday afternoon on the lawn in front of her Pacific Pinnacles apartment, but the smell of the piglet kept Darby from drifting off. She'd already wasted too much time waiting for its parents to show up.

Darby sat up slowly, saw no other pigs, then stood. No tide of dizziness took her back down, so she glanced up the hill at Hoku.

Between her and her horse stood a black pig the size of a Labrador retriever. Two wiggling piglets were there, too.

The sow snorted and the piglet next to Darby scooted away. As he joined the others, Darby noticed he was the smallest.

When the sow led her family trotting away, Darby couldn't help but watch Hoku. Switching her tail lazily, Hoku gazed after the pigs, but she didn't look scared, just interested.

What a totally different reaction than the filly had had to the pig in the corral, Darby thought.

She hadn't imagined it, then. The boar in her camp was a sick animal. Healthy pigs like this bunch moved away from strangers.

As Darby took her first step toward Hoku, the sow stopped and stared.

Does she have eyes in the back of her head? Darby wondered.

The sow had to be at least a quarter-mile away, but Darby heard her grunt a warning to her piglets.

They weren't the least bit worried by Darby or her horse. In fact, the small one was leading a rollicking romp through the grass. At last, their mother trotted after them.

Darby had to get back before Jonah or someone else saw the empty corral and sent out a search party.

Although she had no idea how to return to camp, Hoku did.

So Darby followed along, watching all the while for a clear spring so she could bathe. She knew Hoku would share the stream she drank from in camp, but she wanted to keep it clean for her horse. Besides, the idea of bathing in the stream where the pig had been, and the specter of him lurking nearby to ambush her, wasn't very appealing.

Holding Hoku's lead rope while she washed off didn't make for a very complete bath, but before they crossed the *kipuka*, Darby was pretty much free of mud. Heat waves radiating up from the lava rock provided warmth to counter the wet patches that were left all over her shirt and shoulders from her long hair.

"Would you let me give you a bath?" Darby asked Hoku, but the horse only flicked one ear her way. She was so determined to get back to the corral—and hay—Darby probably could have released the lead rope again and just tagged along. But she wasn't about to try it.

Their camp appeared undamaged and the pig had gone. The only signs he'd ever been there was the ripped-up wallow under the fence and the open gate, blowing and creaking in the breeze.

Hoku wandered around her corral while Darby snagged Jonah's wildlife book off the ground. It was untouched, as if she'd set it carefully on the little knoll, instead of dropping it when she was under attack.

Next, she used a cup from her supplies to bring damp dirt from the streambed. It wouldn't help much if the pig was determined to get under the bottom rail again, but Darby packed mud into the low spot until it was level with the dirt around it.

"That should slow him down," she told Hoku.

Darby brushed her hands against each other, then said, "Let's go see Tutu."

Hoku's head jerked up. Her eyes blinked as she'd come out of a doze, but when Darby tried to lead her, the filly wouldn't move.

"C'mon, girl," Darby coaxed, "we've got to tell her about the pig, and I'm not leaving you here."

Everything Darby had observed made her believe

the black boar was rabid, and horses could get rabies, too.

"We'll walk over to Tutu's, tell her what happened, then go home and tell Jonah. We really don't want Megan to show up tomorrow morning to look for Tango and run into trouble with a boar," she said.

"Hoku!" Darby gave the rope a firm tug. "I can't leave you here alone."

She wouldn't *go* alone, either.

If she were Tutu, she'd insist her great-granddaughter stay safe in the cottage rather than return to territory roamed by a rabid pig, whether there was a horse waiting for her or not.

Darby tried sweet-talking the filly. She tried striding out to the end of the lead rope as if she just assumed the mustang would follow. Hoku didn't move.

She didn't say it aloud, but Darby thought Hoku was acting like horses she'd read about, which stayed in the "safety" of their stalls, refusing to leave even when fire roared around them.

Finally, Darby gave up. They'd leave at first light. By then, Hoku would have recovered.

Darby found a stout branch that had fallen on the rain-forest floor and stripped the leaves from it. That would make a passable club. She'd protect herself and Hoku from the pig if she had to.

I only have to make it through the night, Darby thought. Even a rabid pig must have learned a lesson today. Wouldn't he avoid a place where he'd been stuck under a fence, yelled at by an insane human, and practically trampled by a horse?

The pig didn't come to the stream at dusk. He didn't show up at midnight, either.

Afraid her camping lantern could be dangerous because the boar could stagger into it, spill lantern fuel, and cause a fire, Darby read a book by the beam of her flashlight.

Exhausted and sore, Darby thought she'd have to fight to stay awake, but the opposite was true. She couldn't fall asleep.

Darby flipped through Jonah's book and learned about Hawaii's endangered nene goose. She read the section on feral pigs, too, and one fact kept rising to the surface of her mind long after she'd finished the chapter.

Because of their tough hide and the scar tissue on shoulders, feral pigs can only be killed with bullets, the passage had said.

Megan had been afraid of Cade because he carried a rifle everywhere he went. That's what she'd said. So if Cade had had a rifle that day in the rain forest, why hadn't he used it to save Ben Kato?

The black boar still hadn't shown up at dawn, but Megan, Cade, and Kit did.

Darby heard their approach and struggled into

jeans to cover her skinned knees. Tears filled her eyes by the time she pulled up her zipper and made it into her only wearable shirt.

Yesterday, she'd been surprised that her muscles only ached a little from her smash-and-tear, stumble-and-drag journey at the end of Hoku's rope. But today she ached everywhere. Even her fingernails hurt.

Darby limped to the edge of the clearing. The first thing she noticed was that Megan rode Navigator. Darby didn't have even a second to feel jealous, though. The instant he spotted her, the big gelding tossed his head and gave a short, happy neigh.

Darby blew the Quarter Horse a kiss, then she looked closely at Megan and Cade. The two rode into the clearing side by side. Even though they weren't talking, the silence that had been like a wall of ice between them was clearly melting.

Kit jogged Conch past the others.

"Hey there, cowgirl," said the foreman.

Darby felt a thrill of pride at the greeting and she waved.

Kit Ely held his reins in his right hand, while his left rested on the thigh of his short leather chaps. With his night-black hair and dark skin, he might be mistaken for a Hawaiian, though he was really half Shoshone. But that wasn't what made Kit remarkable.

Darby admired the way he kept Conch quiet. The

grulla gelding was a challenge to Megan, and she was a good rider, but Conch obeyed Kit without question.

Kit rode with such ease, Darby wouldn't have believed he'd been badly injured riding rodeo broncs if she hadn't heard about the accident from a good source.

Kit's left wrist was "dust," according to Sam Forster, and Sam had heard the description from Kit's brother Jake.

"Filly looks fine," Kit said.

He gave Darby a conspiratorial wink. They shared an admiration for mustangs that Jonah didn't have. Her grandfather had said it would take Hoku at least a year to become fit enough to ride, but Kit had believed Hoku's wild-horse toughness would cut the recovery time needed after her voyage and relocation in half.

"'Course," Kit added, smiling at Hoku's excited neighs to the other horses, "she sounds a mite lonesome."

"She's fibbing," Darby said. "She's had Tango for company."

"Has she?" Kit sounded surprised.

Darby wished she hadn't revealed that quite so soon. She didn't want to tell Kit everything that had happened with the pig. At least not yet.

But Kit was an expert tracker. In fact, if she'd given his presence just two minutes of thought, she would have realized he was here to help find Tango.

Kit rode around the outside of the corral, eyes fixed on the ground, then widened his search while Darby went to the others.

Although Megan and Cade had joined forces to recapture Tango, there was still an awkwardness between them.

"You rode," Darby said suddenly.

"Only because Tutu gave us permission," Megan said. "We're allowed to come in on horseback and catch Tango, but Tutu made us promise we wouldn't gallop after her until we'd tried plan A," Megan said.

But then Megan detailed plan B instead.

Joker and Navigator were both good roping horses, Megan explained, and since she and Cade threw lucky loops most of the time, Cade would send Joker galloping after Tango, then put a loop over her head.

"I'll lag behind, so she knows I'm still her friend," Megan said.

"Or you'll be there with a second rope, if I miss my throw," Cade said.

"You won't," Megan said. Then, seeing Darby glance toward Kit, Megan added, "Jonah wants Kit to track that crazy pig you saw. Then, after we catch Tango and all 'us kids' are gone, Jonah expects Kit to come back and kill it."

The idea would have horrified Darby yesterday, but after facing the pig, she wasn't so sure.

"I don't know if he's crazy," Darby said. "But I saw that boar yesterday, and I think it does have rabies."

Cade straightened in his saddle, watching intently as Kit jogged up on Conch.

Right then, Darby noticed Cade wasn't the only one with a scabbard on his saddle.

"Judgin' by tracks, we got one sick hog," Kit said. "Let's get your plan rollin'." He nodded toward Megan. "Horses are our first priority. I want them outta here until I take care of that boar."

Kit's opinion meant she'd had a good reason to be scared yesterday, Darby thought. Then she swallowed and asked Megan, "What's plan A?"

"Bubbles." Megan dismounted with a smile, unbuckled her saddlebag, and took out a plastic jar.

She winked at Darby, confirming that she'd believed what Darby had said: Bubbles had lured Tango here in the first place.

Darby heard Hoku's hooves and looked over to see the filly pacing. The mustang was all lathered up, as if she'd been running.

What's wrong, girl? Darby sent her thoughts toward the sorrel. *Too many people? Too much commotion? Or do you smell trouble?*

"Let's do it." Kit's resolute voice brought Darby's attention back to plans A and B as the foreman scanned the woods around them. "You three can talk while you loosen cinches and tie up the horses. Megan, how about you get out there by the stream in ten minutes?"

"Got it," Megan agreed.

"I'll give you until noon to coax Tango to you. If she doesn't come, then we'll try something else. I want all these horses out of here before dark."

"Then," Megan said carefully, "no offense to anyone, but I think my best chance to catch her is if I'm out there alone."

Everyone nodded, and though Darby longed to watch Megan's reunion with her rose roan mare, she knew the older girl was probably right.

"So, why didn't Jonah come?" Darby asked as she tethered Navigator while Megan loosened his cinch.

Before Megan answered, Cade interrupted, pointing at Darby's elbow.

"What did you do?"

"Gosh, is that down to the bone?" Megan gasped.

"It's nothing," Darby said.

Cupping her hand over the scrape to hide it, she could feel that it had started bleeding again.

"We can fix it real quick," Cade said.

"It doesn't hurt or anything," Darby protested, but she realized Cade had been looking at Kit, assuring the foreman that first aid wouldn't take long.

When Kit nodded, Cade stopped listening to Darby.

Working as quickly as Tutu had while making her antiasthma potion, Cade used his knife to gather some of the fern velvet Jonah had made her touch. Then he pressed it to Darby's elbow and left her holding it in place while he searched for a ti leaf.

"Jonah got into a squabble with his sister, Babe. Your aunt," Megan muttered.

Darby remembered Tutu using her fingertip to draw a line on the tabletop, showing how she'd divided the family lands between Jonah and his sister.

"And then poor Jonah had to stay at Babe's five-star resort to talk things out," Megan said, smirking.

"Oh yeah," Darby said. She vaguely remembered the Sugar Bay or Cove or Something Else Resort that Kimo had pointed out on their drive from the airport to the ranch.

Cade returned holding a broad green leaf and told Darby, "Your tutu did this for me, and it worked real well." He bound the ti leaf over the fern velvet. "Just leave it to heal for a week and you won't even know you were hurt."

"Thanks," Darby said.

Since she'd been banned from watching the execution of plan A, Darby groomed Hoku. It didn't soothe the filly as it usually did, but Darby kept at her brushing for over an hour before she stopped.

Hoku stood with her head low. Sweat darkened the golden hair around her white-starred chest to a yellow-brown.

"This is all just too much, isn't it, girl? First the pig, now all these people, and horses on the other side of the fence while you're inside."

But Hoku's ears didn't prick up to listen to Darby's voice. The mustang just looked at her, dull-eyed.

Megan had settled by the stream with Tango's old halter, hoping the mare would recognize its scent. She blew bubbles, too, and every now and then, the breeze brought Darby the sound of Megan talking.

Cade perched in a tree overlooking the stream, so he could alert Megan if the rustling she heard coming toward her wasn't Tango, but the boar. And though Darby knew which tree he'd climbed, Cade was so still, she couldn't spot him.

Kit rode the perimeter of the *kipuka* without saying if he was looking for the boar or the rose roan. And Darby forgot all about him until she left the corral.

"Come ride with me," Kit said as Darby locked the corral gate behind her.

Without a second thought, Darby agreed. More nervous than achey, she hurried, as fast as her sore legs would carry her, over to Navigator, and resaddled him.

For one moment she was afraid her muscles were too sore to lift her foot into the stirrup, and she yelped as she swung her right leg over Navigator's back, but once she was settled in the saddle, she felt okay.

As they rode, she noticed Kit checking out her scraped elbow, the way she rolled her shoulders to keep them from stiffening, and the careful way she held Navigator's reins to keep them from rubbing her tender palms.

"Is this a setup?" she asked him, surprising herself with her ability to joke with the foreman. "Did you ask me to ride so that you could see if I did something stupid to get myself all banged up?"

"Naw," Kit said, squinting at the landscape ahead. "You can tell me now, or later. I don't care when, exactly, but you're by golly gonna spill the beans."

So Darby told Kit what had happened yesterday.

Maybe he pointed out hoofprints from Hoku and Tango and the pig just to keep her talking longer, Darby thought, or maybe he was trying to teach her something, but she found herself excited to tell someone about her adventure.

When he didn't scold her, she kept talking.

And even though she meant to leave out the part where she rolled down the hill and came to rest in the middle of a family of pigs, she didn't, because then she couldn't have bragged about Hoku coming back to her.

They rode up a hill and rested the horses at the summit. From there, they could see the entire *kipuka*. It really wasn't very big. In fact, when Kit pointed at a tiny valley that funneled past the stream and into the clearing, Darby gasped, "That's Tango!"

"Yep," Kit said. "Standing right where she can watch Megan, but not going any closer. We're wastin' that terrain," he added, but Darby didn't understand what he meant.

As they headed back downhill, Kit said, "Yesterday? That was a lot to handle on your own."

It wasn't quite a reprimand, but Darby told him, "I didn't want to. I tried to go tell Tutu, but Hoku wouldn't leave her corral."

Kit nodded. "Even mustangs get that way, thinking home base is the only safe place to be."

"And when I thought of that pig coming back and trapping her inside . . ." Darby looked over at Kit, but he made no sign of agreement, so she added, "I know I should have gone for help, but I just couldn't leave her."

But maybe Kit had stopped listening.

"That's it," he said, pointing at Darby. "We'll trap Tango just like we trapped that bronc at the Salinas rodeo."

"We will?" Darby asked, but Kit just motioned for her to catch up.

"Let's go," he said. "It's almost noon and I want to cut those two off before they move on to their crazy plan B."

Darby nudged Navigator with her heels and joined Kit in a lope, but then she shouted, hoping he could hear her through the breeze the horses made,

"There's no plan B without Navigator!"

From the shade of his black hat, Kit flashed her a grin. He gave her a thumbs-up sign, too, but they let the horses continue loping, just for the joy of it.

Chapter 13

Kit squatted in the dirt, drawing with a stick. It didn't take long for him to explain that one of the easiest ways to catch a panicked horse was by cornering it.

"All you need's bait—and for that we can put all the saddle horses in the pen with Hoku and feed 'em early—and enough people walking side by side to make a human chain to cut off her escape."

On the map he'd drawn in the dirt, Kit showed them how the little valley funneled past the stream, then opened into the clearing.

Cade, Megan, and Darby nodded in excitement.

"We just lay up real quiet until she has her drink of water at the stream," Kit said, "and when she starts smelling that hay and going to investigate, we move after her, slowly. And when the corral's in sight and Tango's deciding what to do, you"—Kit nodded his head at Megan—"just mosey up and put her halter on."

"Piece of cake," Megan said, and with that reminder, each of the horse trappers grabbed something to eat, then returned to the rain forest to wait for Tango.

It was late afternoon, three o'clock at least, Darby thought. Her thigh and calf muscles trembled as she crouched in the foliage.

And then Hoku warned them that the rose roan was coming.

The filly let loose a ringing neigh that made birds rise crying from the trees. Then Darby felt the ground beneath her tremble as something crashed through the rain forest, coming toward them.

Skittish but excited, Tango loped right past the stream and the humans in hiding. Her ears pricked forward with almost coltish interest.

"Fall in," Kit said in a stage whisper, but Tango's lope had already carried her out of earshot.

The pink mare didn't look back as Cade, Megan, Kit, and Darby walked after her, leaving six feet or so between them. They followed the mare closely enough that they saw her shy at Darby's shelter, then startle at the sight of the corral. She stopped, then sidestepped as Hoku pressed her sorrel face against the corral fence rails.

Navigator, Conch, and Joker joined Hoku at the fence and stared, transfixed by the other horse.

Tango threw her black mane and it slapped back down on her neck. Her nostrils distended as she sniffed the bottom of the gate.

With a frown and silent shrug, Megan looked over at Darby.

"What's she doing?" Megan mouthed, but when Darby curved her index fingers on either side of her nose in—she thought—a perfect imitation of boar tusks, Megan just shook her head in confusion.

Tango raised her head, trying to see the hay inside the corral, until she looked seventeen hands high.

"Now," Kit whispered, gesturing Megan forward.

She carried the leather halter and strolled toward the mare. Tango glanced over her shoulder and turned back to the corral and then she shied, as if she hadn't believed her eyes the first time.

Megan stopped, held her hand out for the pink mare to sniff, and waited. In just a few minutes, the mare approached close enough for Megan to ease the halter on her head. In a few more, Megan led her toward the gate, where Cade, the only other person the roan knew from her captive life, opened it.

Darby watched all of this from the back, but it seemed to her that Megan walked with pride as she gave Tango an openhanded pat on the rump, telling her it was all right to join the other horses.

Tango bolted forward. She looked back as Cade and Megan closed the gate together, but the pink mare didn't seem to mind. She shouldered past Conch and Joker, then stretched her rosy neck to touch noses with Hoku.

Once the lively horses were inside the fence and the humans were outside, Megan and Darby stared at the horses, discussing every move they made.

"She's pretty peppy, but not wild," Darby said.

"Those scars." Megan winced. "And she's got to smell pig all over this place, but she still let me walk right up to her."

There was no way Darby could say what she was thinking. It was too embarrassing, but that didn't mean it wasn't true.

Love could be stronger than fear.

By the look in Megan's eyes, she already knew that.

"Change of plans," Kit said, startling them both. "We're staying put 'til morning."

No one protested or asked questions as Kit explained. "This boar's still moving around. If he has rabies—and it's not a sure thing—he's in the furious stage. What they do then, mostly, is roam. And lose fear. They get real irritable, too. Want to attack anything that moves. Jonah was hoping—"

Kit broke off and Darby wasn't surprised. The foreman rarely said as much as he already had.

"Point is, with it getting dark, those horses"—he

nodded toward Hoku and Tango—"would be too fractious to take through the woods, even on lead lines."

"Fractious? What's fractious?" Megan asked.

"Restless?" Kit suggested.

"So we'll leave them all in the corral together," Cade said, "and hope the boar's not crazed enough to try to get in."

"Yep," Kit agreed.

With Tango, Navigator, Joker, and Conch for roommates, Hoku would be in heaven, Darby thought. She just hoped the filly didn't remember she preferred the tight crush of horses to her human herd of one.

Megan clapped her hands. She looked excited by the unexpected night of camping. "We didn't really plan this as a slumber party, so we didn't bring that much food," she said. "But we can pool what's in our saddlebags with Darby's supplies!"

"Ain't no slumber party," Kit mumbled, looking surprised by Megan's enthusiasm.

"I'll stand watch," Cade volunteered.

"We'll take shifts," Kit said.

"I'm sure we can make a decent dinner, even if"—Megan put her hands on her hips and looked pointedly at Cade and Kit—"the diners are touchy."

Megan was giddy with joy at the reunion with her horse, Darby thought, and she refused to let the grim situation depress her.

Darby shared her jerky and the freeze-dried Peach Pie Pak but kept enough food to last her the rest of the week when she saw Kit breaking two protein bars into halves and Megan mixing up envelopes of powdered drink mix with water from their canteens.

The biggest surprise came from Cade's saddlebags. He'd brought mochi, a dessert he said was made with sweet bean paste and fruit.

"These don't taste like any beans I've ever had," Darby told him. "They're delicious. If strawberry ice cream wasn't cold, this is what it would taste like."

"You're weird," Megan told her.

"They're better when they're just made," Cade said.

Kit stood and prowled around the camp with his rifle, but before Cade could join him, Megan said, "We're like a team of superheroes," she looked at their faces in the brassy light of the lantern.

"Right," Darby said.

"Really," Megan insisted. "You're a horse charmer. Cade can see in the dark—"

"Night vision isn't a superpower," Cade said, lowering his voice as if the praise embarrassed him. "It's mostly hereditary, like my pupils dilate more than some people's, and there's stuff I've learned to do."

"Kit can track anything on four feet, or two, or— have you tried snakes?" Megan called to him.

"Not lately," he said.

"What's your superpower?" Cade asked Megan.

"I'm a superior athlete, of course," Megan said, yawning.

Then she sagged against Darby's shoulder.

Looking down at her friend, Darby thought it was like someone had blown out a candle. Megan was already asleep.

But Darby felt totally awake.

Kit must have noticed, because he assigned her and Cade to take first watch.

"Wake me at midnight," Kit said, then looked down at Megan. "And I'll wake her at four. Hey, Wonder Woman"—Kit jostled Megan's shoulder—"that okay with you?"

Megan mumbled agreement, then squirmed into her sleeping bag.

Left alone, Cade and Darby were quiet until he said, "Do you care if I turn out the lantern?"

"No, but why?" Darby asked.

"To help my night vision. The longer it is since I've looked into light, the better accustomed I am to seein' in the dark."

"Will it work for me, too?" Darby asked, turning the key on the lantern to Off.

"For anybody," Cade said. "Besides, then we can watch for firebugs."

"Like, fireflies?" Darby asked.

"I don't know. *I've* never seen one, but Jonah says he used to see them all the time when he was a kid."

Cade gazed silently into the night for so long, Darby felt compelled to ask, "Cade, if the pig comes, what are you going to do? I mean, in the old days — well, according to Jonah, you're not supposed to kill anything in this forest, right?"

"Your tutu already thought of that," Cade said. Despite the darkness, Darby heard a smile in his voice.

"She did?"

"She told me there's an old Hawaiian saying about the wrongs done by man being atoned for by a pig."

"Atoned for? Like a scapegoat or something?" Darby asked. "That's not fair."

"It's supposed to be like a sacrifice," Cade told her.

The wrongs done by man, Darby repeated silently. What wrongs? Darby wondered, but she didn't ask Cade. What if he thought she blamed him, too, for Ben's death?

Then Darby's attention returned to her great-grandmother. "Do you think she's like a medicine woman?" Darby felt her elbow, with its ti leaf bandage, again.

"I'd call her an herbalist," Cade answered, without asking who Darby was talking about.

"Or a wise woman," Megan piped up drowsily.

As the night deepened, Darby looked up through the trees. Multicolored stars showed between the leaves. Blue, red, and gold lights shone among those that were diamond white. She knew the color differences had something to do with temperature, but right now, it looked to her like someone had tossed a handful of jewels against black velvet.

"If that pig is rabid," Cade said, breaking the quiet again, "it's suffering."

"I know," Darby said. "Yesterday, it wasn't trying to be ferocious. He looked . . ." She drew a breath, glad it was Cade listening. He might not make fun of her for trying to read a pig's feelings from its wrinkled face. "Disoriented. Confused, but like he couldn't stop himself from crashing into the fence and stuff."

Cade shifted. Holding his rifle across his lap, he turned away from Darby, but she could still hear him say, "And if Kit's right, soon the pig won't be able to swallow water."

Darby shivered. If that was true, the pig's death wouldn't be a sacrifice. It would be a mercy.

The boar came at midnight.

Though the horses' worried whinnies said they'd heard him approaching, all four humans were startled by the pig crashing through the rain forest.

Darby hadn't meant to fall asleep, but the breaking brush was what made her eyes pop open.

"I see him," Cade said quietly.

Except for the feverish huffing of the pig, they were all quiet, until Kit said, "You sure belong in this owl clan, Cade. I can only hear 'im."

He started pumping up the lantern, then said, "Forget it. That's a bad idea for keeping our eyes sharp, right?"

Even though Cade was staring toward the corral, with his rifle raised to his shoulder, he nodded.

Darby couldn't make out the boar's color or shape, but she sensed movement.

"It's at that fence again, isn't it?" Darby said.

"Why are you whispering?" Megan asked in a startlingly loud voice. "Give me a spoon and a pan to pound on. We want to scare it away, don't we?"

The pig swung around to face them, but it moved so quickly, its lack of coordination made it fall. They heard it grunting and struggling, and Megan didn't ask again.

"I'd put an end to it, if I could see well enough." Kit sounded frustrated. "But if it's still where you say"—he watched the back of Cade's head, made visible by the pale braid, and saw him nod—"it's already too close to the horses to take a shot."

A shot in the dark, Darby thought, and for the first time she really knew what it meant.

"If he gets in with the horses—" Darby broke off. For all her tenderhearted feelings toward wildlife, and Megan's, too, they were all thinking of the same thing. They'd seen Tango's scars. The boar's curved tusks could inflict terrible damage on silken legs and tendons.

Hearing the boar stagger closer, the horses began a captive stampede, circling their corral at a gallop. Darby couldn't see them, but she heard their hooves running, and their shoulders ramming against the fence.

"They're gonna try to break out," Cade said. "I don't think we have much choice."

Hoku's fierce neigh, the one she'd used on Black Lava, soared over the whinnies of the other horses. Then another neigh joined hers.

"That's Tango," Megan said breathlessly. "I can't tell if she's mad or scared, but—"

They heard hooves hit the fence.

Kit crouched next to Cade and asked, "Are they trying to kick their way out?"

"No," Cade said. "It's Tango and Hoku. They're—" Cade stopped.

"What?" Darby demanded.

"They're going after the pig."

One of the horses screamed in fury, then horseflesh hit horseflesh. Teeth clacked. Darby imagined her mustang filly and the once-wild mare shoving past the geldings to get to the bristled menace coming after them.

Hooves battered against wood.

"Aw." Cade made a pitying sound just before the pig began to shriek.

He pressed his rifle tighter against his shoulder.

The horses' hooves had found their target. The

piercing squeals raised gooseflesh on Darby's arms, but the pig was still shoving against the fence. She heard the wood creak.

"What do you want me to do?" Cade asked sternly.

"If you can see to make a shot, take it," Kit said.

"Darby?" Cade snapped.

"Take it," Kit repeated, "before he gets among the horses."

Darby's mind cast around for a different solution.

If Hoku was in the line of fire, Cade wouldn't shoot, would he? Unless the pig was about to slip under as it had before and attack Navigator, or Joker, or —

"Okay," Darby said.

"Megan." Cade said her name in a steely tone.

If anything went wrong, he wanted her on his side this time, Darby thought.

"Okay. Of course. Do it," Megan said.

Kit's faith in Cade's skill was so great, he was already reaching for the lantern when Cade put the pig out of its misery with a single shot.

The horses stood silent. The only sound was Kit, pumping up the lantern and lighting it.

"Stay here," Kit said, standing up. "You too," he told Cade. "I'm pretty sure he's done for, but I'd feel better if you covered me from here."

Cade nodded, and Kit walked toward the pig.

 Chapter 14

Darby didn't watch while Kit made sure the sick boar was dead, but she listened.

For a few minutes, there was no other sound except for Kit's boots, but then the quiet was split by Hoku's longing neigh.

"Kit!"

"Yeah?"

"Can I go to Hoku?" Darby shouted to him.

"Sure. She's fine, though. The boar didn't get in."

Then, as Darby started toward Hoku, Kit corrected himself. "You know, could you wait just a second while Cade helps me with this?"

"This" would be the boar's body, Darby thought, so she stayed where she was.

Cade stood, but Megan was so fast getting to her feet and grabbing his sleeve, she stopped him from going.

"I apologize for being such a jerk," Megan said.

"It's okay," Cade told her.

"It's not okay," Megan insisted. "That day, you would have shot that boar, and my dad would still be alive—"

"I could have missed. And even shot, he still could've charged Tango and the same thing woulda happened."

"No. I came out of the forest after you and Dad did, and when I saw you with your gun raised, but I didn't see the boar . . ."

"And you screamed for me to stop. But how could you think something like that about me? That I'd do something like that?"

"I don't know. I've always been weird about little animals . . ."

"Little animals." Cade repeated the words as if he'd never heard them before.

"Well, it—I know. I know, looking back it's stupid, but I didn't see the boar and I thought you were going to shoot that baby pig Tango was shying away from." Megan gave a heartsick sigh, then spoke through gritted teeth. "I don't know why."

Darby tried to picture what Cade and Megan had described.

Megan had come into the clearing after the

others. She'd seen Cade—a guy she was afraid of because her mother had told her he'd had violence pounded into him—raise his rifle against a baby pig. But she hadn't seen the boar charging Tango. She hadn't guessed her father was in danger. Still, her scream had stopped Cade from shooting.

Cade's shaky voice broke the silence. "You didn't think I was going to shoot your dad?"

"No! Oh my gosh, Cade, no! I'd never think something like that!"

Then Darby walked away. She headed for her horse, though her head was spinning.

All this time, Megan had blamed herself for shouting, for worrying about a piglet instead of her father.

All this time, Cade had thought Megan, for at least a moment, believed he was aiming at Ben Kato.

Darby circled to the far side of the corral. All of the horses crowded toward her as if she, the hay-bringer, could do something about the chaos that had invaded their world.

"It's okay, you guys," she said quietly. "Everything's going to be just fine."

At first light, Cade and Megan rode out, ponying Tango behind them.

Kit was still worried. He lagged behind, arguing with Darby.

"That pig got rabies from somewhere," he pointed

out, but Darby could tell she was wearing him down. "Still, I know what Jonah would say. He'd tell you there's no reason you can't spend the last couple days out here with your horse, now that the boar's been taken care of. So have a good time," he said, and loped Conch after the others.

When the rain forest fell quiet again, Darby joined Hoku in the corral.

She watched her filly eat the hay meant to distract Hoku from the departure of her temporary herd. She smiled as Hoku rolled in the dirt, then rubbed her coat on the grass, removing all of those troubling scents.

Finally, when Hoku was ready to play, Darby tightened her black ponytail.

Hoku came to her, holding her head up high so that Darby couldn't reach her halter, but when Darby didn't try, the mustang lowered her head over Darby's shoulder and bumped her chin against her shoulder blade in a horse hug.

"I've got something to read to you, girl," Darby said. She wiggled her fingers into her jeans pocket to retrieve the postcard she'd found in the book Jonah had packed for her. It was from her mother.

" 'Don't stay in your room studying,' it says, and then, 'Get out and have some fun!' "

Darby laughed, and she decided Hoku was amused, too, because she dusted her prickly whiskers across Darby's face.

"She has no idea," Darby told Hoku. "And she wouldn't believe me if I told her!"

Hoku tilted her head to one side, trying to puzzle out Darby's words. When she couldn't, the filly shook all over.

A flurry of ivory mane covered Hoku's eyes before she gave Darby a sisterly nudge that knocked her off her feet. And then, head held high and bright tail streaming, the golden mustang ran circles around her human.

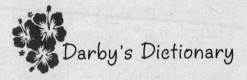 Darby's Dictionary

In case anybody reads this besides me, which it's too late to tell you not to do if you've gotten this far, I know this isn't a real dictionary. For one thing, it's not all correct, and for another, it's not alphabetized because I'm just adding things as I hear them. Besides, this dictionary is just to help me remember. Even though I'm pretty self-conscious about pronouncing Hawaiian words, it seems to me if I live here (and since I'm part Hawaiian), I should at least try to say things right.

'aumakua — OW MA KOO AH — these are family guardians from ancient times. I think ancestors are supposed to come back and look out for their family members. Our 'aumakua are owls and Megan's is a sea turtle.

chicken skin — goose bumps

da kine — DAH KYNE — "that sort of thing" or "stuff like that"

hanai — HA NYE E — a foster or adopted child, like Cade is Jonah's, but I don't know if it's permanent

'iolani — EE OH LAWN EE — this is a hawk that brings messages from the gods, but Jonah has it painted on his trucks as an owl bursting through the clouds

hiapo — HIGH AH PO — a firstborn child, like me, and it's apparently tradition for grandparents, if they feel like it, to just take hiapo to raise!

hoku — HO COO — star

ali'i — AH LEE EE — royalty, but it includes chiefs besides queens and kings and people like that

pupule — POO POO LAY — crazy

<u>paniolo</u> — PAW KNEE OH LOW — cowboy or cowgirl

<u>lanai</u> — LAH NA E — this is like a balcony or veranda. Sun House's is more like a long balcony with a view of the pastures.

<u>lei niho palaoa</u> — LAY NEEHO PAH LAHOAH — necklace made for old-time Hawaiian royalty from braids of their own hair. It's totally kapu—forbidden—for anyone else to wear it.

<u>luna</u> — LOU NUH — a boss or top guy, like Jonah's stallion

<u>pueo</u> — POO AY OH — an owl, our family guardian. The very coolest thing is that one lives in the tree next to Hoku's corral.

<u>pau</u> — POW — finished, like Kimo is always asking, "You pau?" to see if I'm done working with Hoku or shoveling up after the horses

<u>pali</u> — PAW LEE — cliffs

<u>ohia</u> — OH HE UH — a tree like the one next to Hoku's corral

lei — LAY E — necklace of flowers. I thought they were pronounced LAY, but Hawaiians add another sound. I also thought leis were sappy touristy things, but getting one is a real honor, from the right people.

luahala — LOO AH HA LA — some kind of leaf in shades of brown, used to make paniolo hats like Cade's. I guess they're really expensive.

kapu — KAH POO — forbidden, a taboo

tutu — TOO TOO — great-grandmother

menehune — MEN AY WHO NAY — little people

honu — HO NEW — sea turtle

hewa-hewa — HEE VAH HEE VAH — crazy

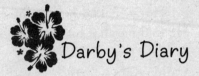 Darby's Diary

Ellen Kealoha Carter—my mom, and since she's responsible for me being in Hawaii, I'm putting her first. Also I miss her. My mom is a beautiful and talented actress, but she hasn't had her big break yet. Her job in Tahiti might be it, which is sort of ironic because she's playing a Hawaiian for the first time and she swore she'd never return to Hawaii. And here I am. I get the feeling she had huge fights with her dad, Jonah, but she doesn't hate Hawaii.

Cade—fifteen or so, he's Jonah's adopted son. Jonah's been teaching him all about being a paniolo. I thought he was Hawaiian, but when he took off his hat he had blond hair—in a braid! Like old-time vaqueros—weird! He doesn't go to school, just takes his classes by correspondence through the mail. He wears this poncho that's almost black it's such a dark green, and he blends in with the forest. Kind of creepy the way he just appears out there. Not counting Kit, Cade might be the best rider on the ranch.

Hoku kicked him in the chest. I wish she hadn't. He told me that his stepfather beat him all the time.

<u>Cathy Kato</u>—forty or so? She's the ranch manager and, really, the only one who seems to manage Jonah. She's Megan's mom and the widow of a paniolo, Ben. She has messy blond-brown hair to her chin, and she's a good cook, but she doesn't think so. It's like she's just pulling herself back together after Ben's death.

I get the feeling she used to do something with advertising or public relations on the mainland.

<u>Jonah Kaniela Kealoha</u>—my grandfather could fill this whole notebook. Basically, though, he's harsh/nice, serious/funny, full of legends and stories about magic, but real down-to-earth. He's amazing with horses, which is why they call him the Horse Charmer. He's not that tall, maybe 5'8", with black hair that's getting gray, and one of his fingers is still kinked where it was broken by a teacher because he spoke Hawaiian in class! I don't like his "don't touch the horses unless they're working for you" theory, but it totally works. I need to figure out why.

<u>Kimo</u>—he's so nice! I guess he's about twenty-five, Hawaiian, and he's just this sturdy, square, friendly guy. He drives in every morning from his house over by Crimson Vale, and even though he's late a lot, I've never seen anyone work so hard.

<u>Kit Ely</u>—the ranch foreman, the boss, next to Jonah. He's Sam's friend Jake's brother and a real buckaroo. He's about 5'10" with black hair. He's half Shoshone, but he could be mistaken for Hawaiian, if he wasn't always promising to whip up a batch of Nevada chili and stuff like that. And he wears a totally un-Hawaiian leather string with brown-streaked turquoise stones around his neck. He got to be fore-man through his rodeo friend Pani (Ben's buddy). Kit's left wrist got pulverized in a rodeo fall. He's still amazing with horses, though.

<u>Megan Kato</u>—Cathy's fifteen-year-old daughter, a super athlete with long reddish-black hair. She's beau-tiful and popular and I doubt she'd be my friend if we just met at school. Maybe, though, because she's nice at heart. She half makes fun of Hawaiian legends, then turns around and acts really serious about them. Her Hawaiian name is Mekana.

<u>The Zinks</u>—they live on the land next to Jonah. They have barbed-wire fences and their name doesn't sound Hawaiian, but that's all I know.

<u>Tutu</u>—my great-grandmother. She lives out in the rain forest like a medicine woman or something, and she looks like my mom will when she's old. She has a pet owl.

❧ ANIMALS! ❧

<u>Hoku</u>—my wonderful sorrel filly! She's about two and a half years old, a full sister to the Phantom, and boy, does she show it! She's fierce (hates men) but smart, and a one-girl (ME!) horse for sure. She is definitely a herd-girl, and when it comes to choosing between me and other horses, it's a real toss-up. Not that I blame her. She's run free for a long time, and I don't want to take away what makes her special.

She loves hay, but she's really HEAD-SHY due to Shan Stonerow's early "training," which, according to Sam, was beating her.

Hoku means "star." Her dam is Princess Kitty, but her sire is a mustang named Smoke and he's mustang all the way back to a "white renegade with murder in his eye" (Mrs. Allen).

<u>Navigator</u>—my riding horse is a big, heavy Quarter Horse that reminds me of a knight's charger. He has Three Bars breeding (that's a big deal), but when he picked me, Jonah let him keep me! He's black with rusty rings around his eyes and a rusty muzzle. (Even

though he looks black, the proper description is brown, they tell me.) He can find his way home from any place on the island. He's sweet, but no pushover. Just when I think he's sort of a safety net for my beginning riding skills, he tests me.

Joker Cade's Appaloosa gelding is gray splattered with black spots and has a black mane and tail. He climbs like a mountain goat and always looks like he's having a good time. I think he and Cade have a history, maybe Jonah took them in together?

Biscuit — buckskin gelding, one of Ben's horses, a dependable cowpony. Kit rides him a lot.

Hula Girl — chestnut cutter

Blue Ginger — blue roan mare with tan foal

Honolulu Lulu — bay mare

Tail Afire (Koko) — fudge brown mare with silver mane and tail

Blue Moon — Blue Ginger's baby

Moonfire — Tail Afire's baby

<u>Black Cat</u>—Lady Wong's black foal

<u>Luna Dancer</u>—Hula Girl's bay baby

<u>Honolulu Half Moon</u>

<u>Conch</u>—grulla cowpony, gelding, needs work. Megan rides him sometimes.

<u>Kona</u>—big gray, Jonah's cow horse

<u>Luna</u>—beautiful, full-maned bay stallion is king of 'Iolani Ranch. He and Jonah seem to have a bond.

<u>Lady Wong</u>—dappled gray mare and Kona's dam. Her current foal is Black Cat.

<u>Australian shepherds</u>—pack of five and I have to learn their names!

<u>Pipsqueak/Pip</u>—little, shaggy, white dog that runs with the big dogs, belongs to Megan and Cathy.

<u>Tango</u>—Megan's, once-wild rose roan mare. I think she and Hoku are going to be pals.

❧ PLACES ❧

<u>Lehua High School</u>—the school Megan goes to and I will, too. School colors are red and gold.

<u>Crimson Vale</u>—it's an amazing and magical place, and once I learn my way around, I bet I'll love it. It's like a maze, though. Here's what I know: from town you can go through the valley or take the ridge road—valley has lily pads, waterfalls, wild horses, and rainbows. The ridge route (Pali?) has sweeping turns that almost made me sick. There are black rock teeter-totter-looking things that are really ancient altars and a SUDDEN drop-off down to a white sand beach. Hawaiian royalty are supposedly buried in the cliffs.

<u>Moku Lio Hihiu</u>—Wild Horse Island, of course!

<u>Mountain to the Sky</u>—sometimes just called Sky Mountain. Goes up to 5,000 feet, sometimes gets snow, and Megan said there used to be wild horses there.

<u>The Two Sisters</u>—cone-shaped "mountains." A borderline between them divides Jonah's land from his sister's—my aunt, but I haven't met her. One of them is an active volcano. Kind of scary.

<u>Sun House</u>—our family place. They call it plantation style, but it's like sugar plantation, not Southern mansion. It has an incredible lanai that overlooks pastures all the way to Mountain to the Sky and Two Sisters. Upstairs is this little apartment Jonah built for my mom, but she's never lived in it.

<u>Hapuna</u>—biggest town on island, has airport, flagpole, public and private schools, etc., palm trees, and coconut trees

<u>'Iolani Ranch</u>—our home ranch. 2,000 acres, the most beautiful place in the world.

❧ ON THE RANCH, THERE ARE ❧
PASTURES WITH NAMES LIKE:

<u>Sugar Mill</u> and <u>Upper Sugar Mill</u>—for cattle

<u>Two Sisters</u>—for young horses, one- and two-year-olds they pretty much leave alone

<u>Flatland</u>—mares and foals

<u>Pearl Pasture</u>—borders the rain forest, mostly two- and three-year-olds in training

<u>Borderlands</u>—saddle herd and Luna's compound

I guess I should also add me . . .

<u>Darby Leilani Kealoha Carter</u> — I love horses more than anything, but books come in second. I'm thirteen, and one-quarter Hawaiian, with blue eyes and black hair down to about the middle of my back. On a good day, my hair is my best feature. I'm still kind of skinny, but I don't look as sickly as I did before I moved here. I think Hawaii's curing my asthma. Fingers crossed.

I have no idea what I did to land on Wild Horse Island, but I want to stay here forever.

Darby and Hoku's adventures continue in . . .

CASTAWAY COLT

 Castaway Colt

Black sand muffled the sound of Navigator's hooves as he trotted toward the ocean.

Head flung high, the brown gelding breathed the salt of waves lapping up on Night Digger Point Beach.

Darby Carter could hardly believe her eyes. She'd grown up near the beach in California, but she'd never seen black sand. Did people who'd been raised on Hawaiian islands look at black sand as an everyday thing?

"Just another day in paradise," Darby joked to her horse. "And you're already barefooted."

Darby couldn't wait to take off her riding boots and feel the millions of dark crystals work up between her toes, while she gazed out at the ocean.

Ever since Megan, Darby's first friend in Hawaii, had described Night Digger Point Beach, Darby had been eager to see it.

Today, the last day before starting her new school, was a great occasion to explore this black-sand beach.

The only thing that would have made the day just right, was if she could have brought Hoku, her mustang, along with her. Darby had just spent a week in the rain forest with Hoku, and now she couldn't bear being away from the filly.

Begging to bring Hoku along because she loved her would not convince her grandfather, Jonah, to allow it. So she tried a more sensible approach.

"Wouldn't it be good training for me to pony Hoku to the beach? And if we had any little adventures"—Darby drew a quick breath, hoping Jonah wouldn't think of strange stallions and wild pigs before she went on—"Hoku could learn from Navigator how to act."

To Darby, it had sounded like an excellent proposal, but Jonah hadn't seen it her way.

"What you call adventure, I call bad planning," Jonah had answered. "And the filly's too green to be mixed up in more of it."

"But—"

"You and Navigator have a good time, because there's work waiting for you when you get back,"

Jonah had said. "Unless you want to start right now."

Darby had been about to protest that she'd finished all her chores when she caught the direction of Jonah's gaze.

He'd squinted pointedly toward Hoku's corral. There, the sorrel filly had touched noses over the fence with an old bay gelding named Judge.

Darby knew what that look meant, so she'd ridden away on Navigator.

Only now did she confide in her horse. "I don't know if what he wants is possible. Hoku lived as a wild horse. What do you think?" she asked, absently working her fingers through Navigator's black mane while she gazed at the beach. "Can I make her loyal to me over you guys?"

Darby smiled as Navigator feinted a nip toward her stirrup.

"Does that mean you're not into scenery?" she asked her horse, but Navigator turned back toward the waves with pricked ears.

It looked like another world, a magical realm named for the night-digging sea turtles that used it as a nursery.

Megan had had to go to school today, but she'd promised Darby that they'd pack a picnic supper on the Fourth of July, trek to this beach, and spend the night watching mother turtles dig black-sand cradles for their eggs.

Darby sighed. It sounded like fun, but this was

April. She didn't know how much longer she'd be on Wild Horse Island. The Fourth of July seemed a long way off.

Navigator neighed, pawed up a shower of sand, then pulled at his bit, telling Darby he wanted to lope into the waves.

"No, the tide's coming in," Darby told her horse.

She could body surf and swim. She could spot riptides and escape their attempts to drag her out to sea, but she'd climbed on a horse for the very first time just a few weeks ago. Riding waves on a boogie board was one thing; riding them on a horse was a test she wasn't ready for. Yet.

But then Darby noticed a foam-filled depression on top of a big rock. She estimated it was only five or six horse lengths away and only as high as Navigator's back.

As the foam turned into a mirror-clear surface, Darby longed to explore a Hawaiian tide pool and see if it had anemones, mussels, and little fish like the tide pools in Southern California.

"If I ground-tie you, you'll stay put. Right?" Darby asked Navigator.

She imagined dismounting, tugging off her boots, and picking her way up that slippery, truck-sized rock to the tide pool.

Waves rolled in and splashed over the boulder. Seawater filled the pool and overflowed in bubbly streamers.

As spray drifted on the breeze, misting Darby's face, she told herself the waves' impact wouldn't be enough to knock her off her feet.

Her toes curled inside her boots, reminding her how to cling barefooted to wet and riddled rocks.

Darby stood in her stirrups for a better view of the tide pool.

It was perfectly round.

"Either it was made with a giant ice-cream scoop," Darby told Navigator, "or a bubble popped there when the lava was cooling."

The big gelding stood still, his muscles tensed beneath the saddle, but Darby didn't think he was listening to her.

"Do you smell something interesting? Or see—" Darby stopped whispering.

She saw it, too.

Something moved. The creature must be balanced on a ledge in the seaward side of the rock. It was white as the sea foam. Maybe a giant bird?

But wait. That wasn't a wing.

No, a feathery *tail* switched over there. And it was followed by a colt-sized bottom.

Darby gave a surprised laugh. She'd only lived on 'Iolani Ranch for a few weeks, but she knew horses pulled themselves up with their front legs first.

Not this little horse, she corrected herself.

The foal obviously did things his own way. And his way of standing up wasn't the most startling difference about him.

Wind blew tufts of fuzzy mane into curls as the colt turned toward Darby. He studied her with wide, turquoise eyes.

Navigator made a determined yank at the bit, and this time Darby let him move closer.

Hey, little guy. Darby aimed her silent words toward the colt, but she didn't speak. If he was a wild horse, born into the herd in Crimson Vale, he might spook at her human sounds. He could bolt into the ocean.

Navigator's strides stopped at the edge of the truck-sized rock.

Excitement switched Darby's senses on high. She saw the colt wasn't a new baby. At a guess, he was three or four months old, and his coat was a color not found in a box of crayons.

A blush of palomino shimmered among the colt's white hairs, reminding her of waxy white honeycomb.

His blue eyes were flecked with green.

So that's why they look turquoise, Darby thought. And though she'd read that many white mammals were blind at birth, the colt stared at her through a fringe of white eyelashes, telling her he could see her just fine.

The colt's narrow face reminded her of a Thoroughbred's. His rotating ears were the size of Darby's cupped hands, telling her he'd be a towering stallion someday.

But now he whisked his feather-duster tail side to side, and picked his sure-footed way around the volcanic rock.

Stopping just a few yards away, he pointed his pink nose up at Navigator and sniffed, considering horse and rider from this new angle.

"Hi, baby," Darby whispered, since he seemed unafraid.

Suddenly, Navigator backed up. The colt might be fearless, but Navigator's move slammed Darby against the saddle's cantle. Her free arm swung behind her and she flattened her palm against the gelding's rump to steady herself.

"What's up?" she asked Navigator as he kept retreating from the colt.

The little creature followed, making jabs with its nose.

Navigator sidestepped the lips fluttering toward him.

"Are you hungry, baby?" Darby asked.

The white colt was searching for a meal. Navigator's nicker was gentle, but it was definitely a refusal.

"I'm afraid Navigator can't feed you," Darby said, but the white colt wasn't discouraged. He trotted after the gelding.

Darby surveyed the shore. Where was the colt's mother? She saw no mare and heard no worried whinny over the rushing waves.

When the colt's spindly legs brought him near enough, he nudged Navigator's ticklish flank. The gelding snorted.

The colt was so close, Darby could have leaned down and put him off with a push.

Instead, she touched her heels to Navigator's sides, and the relieved gelding jogged off a few strides.

Darby looked over her shoulder in time to see the colt give a frisky buck before he trotted after Navigator. Then, he nipped at the gelding's tail.

"You're in awfully good spirits for an orphan," Darby said. Then she patted Navigator's neck. "And you're a good boy for putting up with him."

The colt kept following them.

This is great, Darby thought. If he trailed after them all the way back to the ranch, someone might recognize him. Or, Auntie Cathy could phone their neighbors.

Who *wouldn't* notice if they'd lost a cream-colored colt with turquoise eyes?

Darby gave a celebratory bounce in her saddle.

She'd almost ruled out the possibility that the colt was the offspring of the wild horses in Crimson Vale.

It wasn't impossible, but in Nevada, Hoku's range-land home, Darby had learned that wild horses knew safety was with the herd. Maybe this little colt had been separated from his band long enough that he'd decided Navigator and he could be a two-horse herd.

Darby shrugged, trying to piece together another reason for the colt to be alone. Maybe he *was* tame. He could have been wading in the shallows with his mother when a strong wave knocked him off his hooves.

After all, she'd just been thinking the waves might knock her down.

Too small to win against the currents, the colt could have been washed ashore here, on Night Digger Point Beach.

Or maybe he belonged to 'Iolani Ranch. He might have slipped out of the broodmare pasture. But she'd ridden those pastures for hours, memorizing the horses and their names, and she didn't recall a blue-eyed colt.

"Keep tagging along," Darby called back to the colt, and he did. For about ten minutes.

When Darby heard the crunch of sand, she looked back. The colt had stopped, folded his legs, and curled up in the sea grass. His head nodded until his whiskers touched his bent knees. Then, he fell asleep.

Darby waited, and Navigator took the time to swing his head around to study this new annoyance.

Darby looked the colt over, too. He wasn't the cutest baby ever born, but once he grew into his head and hooves, he'd be a sleek, white beauty.

"You'll turn into a swan," Darby whispered, and the sound was enough to wake the colt from his nap.

"Let's go," Darby said.

Navigator moved into a swinging walk, but the colt was even friskier and more of a bother to the big horse. Openmouthed, he darted after the gelding.

Darby clucked to her horse, but the colt had already grabbed Navigator's tail.

"Your mom hasn't taught you manners yet, has she?" Darby asked.

Navigator stomped and whisked his black tail away from the colt's mouth.

"He's telling you that's a good way to get kicked," Darby warned as Navigator moved on.

To judge by his pretty prancing, the colt's feelings weren't hurt. Darby would have laughed, if the colt's milk teeth hadn't clamped down hard on Navigator's tail, again.

This time, the gelding couldn't flick his tail loose.

Navigator's head swung around. Eyes narrowed, he clacked his teeth within inches of the colt's face, until he gave up his hold.

Darby did her best to settle into the calm state of mind that had always helped her to read horses.

Letting her eyelids sag and shoulders soften, Darby tried to be receptive.

What's wrong, little one? Like a flower opening to the sun, she was taking in all she could about the colt when he let loose a whinny so shrill, it soared over the rushing of waves and fluttering of leaves.

The pale foal cried out in victory, not fear, and

Darby decided that, though he might be hungry and lonely, he might also be a bit of a brat.

"Don't pull so hard," Darby scolded the colt, but when he zoomed in an excited circle around Navigator, she couldn't be mad at him.

Please don't belong to anyone else, Darby thought.

Of course it was greedy to pretend Navigator, Hoku, *and* this white sea-fairy of a foal would make up her own personal herd of horses, but Darby imagined that very thing.

Her daydreams were interrupted by a squeaky sound. She quickly recognized it as just a loose board in the old plantation house that was falling into ruins in the jungle. But when she looked back to speak a reassuring word, the colt was gone.

Discover all the adventures on
Wild Horse Island!

Phantom Stallion: Wild Horse Island #1: The Horse Charmer

Darby Carter has always loved horses, but as a city girl she's never actually been able to ride. So imagine the thrill when she finds out her grandfather owns a horse ranch! In Hawaii—on a tiny island called Wild Horse Island. It turns out that not only will Darby's granddad take her in but he's going to adopt the mustang Darby helped save. So now Darby is off to Wild Horse Island, ready to meet her horse, and begin the adventure of a lifetime....

Phantom Stallion: Wild Horse Island #2: The Shining Stallion

Darby and her mustang, Hoku, encounter a shadowy horse prowling the ranch at night. Could it be the legendary Shining Stallion of Hawaii—and is he out to challenge the wrong horse? Only Darby can stop him—before anyone gets hurt!

HarperTrophy®
An Imprint of HarperCollins*Publishers*

www.harpercollinschildrens.com